The Man Without a Transit Pass

and other tales

Paradise Edition No. 1
*

ISBN: 979-8-9875626-0-4
Cover Image by R. Adámek

Jaroslav Hašek

**

The Man Without a Transit Pass

and
other tales

***

In a Translation
by

Dustin Stalnaker

***

Paradise Edition No. 1
MMXXIII

This book is dedicated to Grete Reiner
(1889-1944)
pioneering translator of Czech literature.

Contents

A Word About This Collection

The stories collected in this book are relay translations, adapted from Czech into English through German. The translator and editor acknowledge the limitations of this method. Every time a translation is attempted, there is a chance for error. And like the game of telephone—a common but apt metaphor—those errors can be compounded by an intermediary language. Wherever possible, we have compared different versions and consulted with Slavic-language translators and scholars on difficult points. Nevertheless, the basic method remains far from ideal. We welcome informed critiques and corrections to this work.

There is a degree of historical irony in translating Hašek from these sources, though his connection to German language and culture was complex and varied over time. He lived most of his life as a restive subject of the Austro-Hungarian Empire, at a time when Czechs of diverse political and social backgrounds were defining themselves against the government in Vienna. Under Austrian rule, German was the language of the cultural, political, and economic elite, an elite that Hašek ridiculed relentlessly. "The Reform Efforts of Baron Kleinhampl", included in this collection, provides a representative example of his satire on the subject. For his own part, Hašek spoke and wrote German with varying degrees of fluency. Prior to his career as a writer, inexperience with the language cost him a pharmacist's apprenticeship. Later, while residing in Russia during the Bolshevik Revolution, he contributed to the German-language revolutionary newspaper *Sturm*.

Though he wrote primarily in Czech, Hašek was a member of a polyglot society, switching between various languages throughout daily life. The same can be said of his audience, everyday readers of the popular press, who were nonetheless expected to understand cultural references from across Eastern and Central Europe. In the original versions of the stories collected here, there are passages of untranslated Polish, German, and Hungarian. Ethnic relations across the Empire were often tense and competitive, liable to devolve into violence, a state of affairs which led to the outbreak of the First World War and the subsequent dissolution of Austria-Hungary. Hašek used these tensions as fodder for many of his stories, such as the border dispute between the Poles and Hungarians in "The Rescue Mission". But he did not write as an ethnic partisan. Instead of confining his criticism to any particular party or group, Hašek opposed nationalism and chauvinism on principle. He aimed his satire at all sides, his fellow Czechs included.

Translations by German Bohemians played a pivotal role in winning Hašek posthumous acclaim and an international audience. With encouragement from Max Brod (best known today as the editor and literary executor of Franz Kafka), Grete Reiner completed the first translation of Hašek's famed comic novel, *The Good Soldier Švejk*, in 1926. Reiner's German text then served as the basis for the earliest translations of the novel into other languages, as well as for popular stage and film adaptations. Reiner also translated a number of Hašek's short stories. Her versions of "A Legitimate Business", "Money Troubles", "The Footrace", and "The Story of a Respectable Person" serve as sources for this book. Reiner's translations came at a time when Hašek's political message was taking on a new sense of urgency. With the rise of fascism in Europe, his disdain for authority and penchant for iconoclasm won him popularity among left-wing audiences. In the decades before the outbreak of the Second World War, Švejk and his creator became icons for resistance movements across Europe, inspiring writers and artists such as Bertolt Brecht, Arthur Koestler, George Grosz, and John Heartfield. Tragically, such warnings could not prevent the rise of Nazism or the subsequent German occupation of an independent Czechoslovakia in 1938-9. The antifascist message that many took from *Švejk* became pretext for fascist oppression, and the works of Hašek were banned in the nation of his birth. Reiner, a Jew and the editor of a left-wing newspaper in Prague, was deported in 1943 and killed at Auschwitz. It is in her memory that this book is dedicated.

Alongside the cultural history and political values that Hašek shared with his German Bohemian translators, there are stylistic reasons for going through with a relay translation. Hašek held a skeptical attitude toward literature as high art, cutting against contemporary trends of modernist complexity and formal experimentation. He valued humor, storytelling, and political messaging over sophisticated literary constructions. An inspired hack, a tabloid sensationalist, Hašek was prolific but often wrote carelessly, motivated by sheer enthusiasm and raw financial need. His work is riddled with awkward syntax and unintentional ambiguity. In our case, some of this might be attributable to German intermediaries, but translators from Czech are faced with the same problems. Cecil

Parrott, who produced the first full-length version of *Švejk* in English, maintained that anyone translating Hašek should be prepared to revise his writing. And though we sought to minimize our own editorial interventions, we have deferred to this informed judgment. Fidelity is a paramount virtue in translation, but it has to serve some definite end. Hašek gladly bent the truth for the sake of entertainment and self-promotion. He might not mind some expediency.

In any case, Hašek did not write for scholars or for connoisseurs of literary obscura. Despite admiration from figures such as Brod, he was a firm populist. He desired the broadest possible audience. But though he wrote what would become the most popular book in the Czech language, the majority of his work remains, in English at least, untranslated. His essays and short stories have typically been regarded as "minor" compared to *Švejk*. Certainly much of his writing, once topical, has become obscure in the century following his death. The Austro-Hungarian Empire is long gone. But the stories collected here still crackle with the outrageous wit and social conscience that made Hašek famous. He is now firmly within the public domain, available to anyone with the desire and wherewithal to translate him.

So let's raise a glass to Hašek, a pilsner perhaps—the price is right—and spread a good word or two.

The Man Without
a Transit Pass

The Imperial and Royal Transit Authority has always reserved the right to recover any losses it sustains, and it pursues this financial redress with all the rigor of the law.

An incident that occurred on the line running between Říčany and Prague offers a case in point.

One day, an unremarkable man boarded tram car № 16862 of the express service at Uhříněves Station, doing so just as the tram was preparing to depart. Upon the tram's departure, the old, seasoned conductor counted the number of passengers and determined that there were exactly thirty-five people in car № 16862.

The incident unfolded like a tragedy. Namely, as the conductor inspected transit passes at Hostivař station, he noticed that there were only thirty-four people in car № 16862. Convinced that someone must be on the toilet, he carried out a general inspection, in the course of which he indeed established that a man had shut himself away in the lavatory. Upon being prompted to produce his transit pass, the man declared that he was not in a position to do so, because he had arrived at Uhříněves Station only after the ticket office had already closed.

But the regulations applicable to passengers are spelled out quite clearly: should anyone board a tram without a transit pass, he must report this to the conductor immediately, otherwise the lack of a transit pass makes him guilty of fare evasion.

The man offered his apologies, saying that he surely would have done so, had he not suddenly felt a human stirring in his bowels—or, as it is often said, the tummy—which compelled him to seek out the lavatory in great haste. However, it was there that he was discovered by the conductor, who sniffed out an attempt to swindle our noble state out of 50 heller—that is to say, the cost of a transit pass from Uhříněves to Prague.

"We shall explain this to you more thoroughly in Hostivař," the conductor said dryly. And sure enough, upon their arrival the stationmaster turned up and prompted the man without a transit pass to accompany him into his office.

As the train traveled onward, the man without a transit pass was subjected to a thorough interrogation. This interrogation took place in the presence of a gendarme, who had been summoned expressly for this purpose. Making an extraordinarily stern face, the gendarme said "This will cost you dearly. You won't soon forget me!"

But the man without a transit pass stood by his story and stated that he would not pay the fine of five crowns (ten times the price of the transit pass). He conducted himself at all times like a person who was cognizant of his own innocence.

This made an unfavorable impression on the gendarme in particular. He jotted down all sorts of things in his red notebook and remarked sarcastically, "So you hid yourself from the conductor in the lavatory, with the intent of reaching Prague as a stowaway!" But the man without a transit pass always repeated the same story: he did not have time to report to the conductor that he had found the ticket office closed; he had only just boarded the tram when it began to move; he had also promptly asked his fellow passengers where he might alight. He called upon God as his witness that—had his tummy not pained him so—he would have sought out the conductor himself and informed him that he was without a transit pass, because the ticket counter was closed, and he would have requested a transit pass from him. He firmly refused to pay the fine. In fact, he was not willing to pay even the 50 heller for the journey from Uhříněves to Prague, because he had been removed from the tram two stops before reaching his destination. He went so far as to display an abundance of cash, saying that he was entirely capable of paying the fine and was even prepared to do so—were he aware of having committed any offense. Eventually, he declared resolutely that he would pay nothing more than the fare from Uhříněves to Hostivař.

The gendarme then took him to the gendarmerie, where legal proceedings were initiated. The files were then sent to the courts.

The public prosecutor's office swooped in on the affair like a hawk and filed a charge of fraud against the man without a transit pass.

Nor was the Imperial and Royal Transit Authority in Prague remiss in their duties. They wrote, in connection with this matter, to the head transit office in Vienna. At the same time, files containing the interrogation proceedings, led by the conductor of tram car № 16862, as well as those from the stationmasters of Hostivař and Uhříněves, were all handed over to this higher authority. The head office in Vienna reported the incident to the Ministry of Transit, requesting that the Transit Authority in Prague be provisionally entrusted with the investigation into the case, so that the man without a transit pass be condemned to pay, in accordance with existing statutes, both the fine of five crowns and the reimbursement of the 50-heller sum that he had actually cost the Transit Authority in damages. The Ministry of Transit approved the request of the head office in Vienna, to the effect that the Transit Authority in Prague should insist on payment from the man without a transit pass in the amount of 50 heller, for the transit pass from Uhříněves to Prague, and the Ministry was prepared to authorize the deployment of a task force to this end.

In the meantime, the charge of fraud against the man without a transit pass was brought to trial. The man again offered the excuse of stomach pains, and the court regarded this to be a credible alibi and exonerated the defendant.

With this, the Transit Authority had lost their case. However, the public prosecutor lodged an appeal against the decision. The spokesman for the transit administration also protested the ruling and proposed an on-site inspection, namely a survey of the lavatory by a designated task force.

The brain trust of the Transit Authority in Prague promptly shared this proposal with the head office in Vienna, whose executive committee, upon consultation with the head of the Ministry of Transit, granted permission for the creation of a task force. Its purpose was to ascertain whether the man without a transit pass could have made the journey from Kuří to Říčany, during the time of day in question, without reaching Uhříněves station too late—the excuse that he had offered. Moreover, the Ministry of Transit authorized the creation of a second task force responsible for investigating the truth of the statement by the man without a transit pass: that he had already done his business when the conductor opened the door to the lavatory in which he was found at Hostivař; that the conductor was therefore misconstruing the situation when he declared that he had discovered him fully dressed, and that it was not possible that he had done his business in so short a time after having spoken with his fellow passengers.

Both task forces were constituted on the 22nd of July. The review of the matters assigned to them was concluded on the 28th of August. Each task force was comprised of twenty-five research analysts and three engineers.

The task forces cost the state a total of 2,866 crowns. Their findings yielded the following conclusions: after thorough investigation into the matter, it had been found that the man without a transit pass could have reached the ticket office at Uhříněves with sufficient time, prior to closing, and purchased the proper 50-heller ticket to Prague. Furthermore, it was entirely out of the question that the man could have done his business in the short time that he spent in the lavatory of tram car № 16862, as the members of the task force could attest on the basis of their own attempts to do so; his excuses were therefore not credible, and cheating the state out of 50 heller had clearly been his sole intent.

However, in the course of the appeal proceedings, the appellate court upheld the judgment that had found the man without a transit pass innocent, and any remaining hope the transit system had of collecting the 50 heller now lay in civil action.

The incident cost the Imperial and Royal Transit Authority a grand total of 3,678 crowns and 69 heller, and a new fare hike therefore seems inevitable.

1911

I Make Soft-Boiled Eggs

I have a lovely old aunt. Every once in a while, she is gripped by feelings of affection for her kinsfolk. For some fifteen years I had not heard from her, when suddenly the postman delivered a package that she had sent her nephew in one such affectionate mood.

The last time, over fourteen years ago, she sent me a massive cake, and this time the postman delivered a giant basket. In it were found threescore of eggs, along with the touching letter that follows:

Dear Nephew!

How pleased I am to be able to send you threescore of eggs from my own henhouse! Dear lad, I care for you very much, and so I thought to myself, since I probably won't be on this earth much longer, that this is perhaps the final grace that I might bestow upon you. Prepare them yourself, soft-boiled, and remember your old aunt Anna! May these sixty eggs evoke memories of the small plot of land in the north country, on which hens cluck merrily and you are remembered.

Your very loving aunt,
Anna

Out of respect for my aunt, I resolved to prepare all sixty eggs soft-boiled.

At night I even dreamt of it.

In my entire life, I had never concerned myself with the question of how one prepares soft-boiled eggs, but after lengthy contemplation, I arrived at the view that, if one desires to soft boil them, then one must certainly boil them. This seemed to me the only possible angle and my sole recourse, being in such a difficult position as mine: needing to soft boil sixty eggs.

I very much enjoy eating soft-boiled eggs. However, because I nevertheless cannot eat sixty soft-boiled eggs in one sitting, I was plagued by the thought of how to preserve them. Long did I contemplate how to execute this plan.

I Make Soft-Boiled Eggs

Suddenly I found myself in a very tricky situation. I know that young wives are often lampooned in newspapers and other printed matter for not even being able to boil an egg. However, nothing has yet been written about the need of an old bachelor to boil eggs, and for this reason I wish to offer a factual portrayal of how it played out.

To begin, I purchased various books on the rearing of chickens, as I assumed that there, of all places, I would find instructions on how one boils an egg.

Sadly, in all of this technical literature on the rearing of chickens there was not to be found a single place where this theme was given attention. There was indeed much to be read in these texts regarding eggs: for instance, that chicks hatch out of eggs, and other such nonsense. It was also indicated therein, next to instructions on how to incubate eggs, that eggs are to be kept dry. However, because my aunt sent me the eggs with the instruction that they were to be soft boiled, rather than incubated, I reluctantly closed the book.

I did not wish to trouble acquaintances with the question of how eggs are boiled, so I resolved to go to a library and seek out an encyclopedia.

Under the letter "E", keyword "Eggs", I found the note that they are a product of the animal kingdom and that all birds lay eggs. I reflected on this at length. This notion was in no way new to me, but having now seen it in black and white, its credibility was nevertheless increased. It is therefore not simply a figment of folk tradition; scholarship explicitly affirms this notion and backs it up with an entire article.

I investigated further into how eggs are boiled. One desires not to think so complicated a matter has been overlooked by the scientific community. Yet nowhere are any particulars to be found about it.

In the encyclopedia, I came across only the statement that eggs are served as a dish and can be prepared in various ways, but how one goes about preparing these dishes remained an enigma to me, even after being absorbed in the encyclopedia for three hours.

I found only a few sentences that touched on this question from afar. For instance: "In England, eggs are used for nourishment in a variety of raw or cooked states, hard- or soft-boiled. In no proper English household may a soft-boiled egg be missing from the breakfast table. Soft-boiled eggs are generally suitable for every occasion." However, of how one goes about bringing eggs of this kind to the table, I learned nothing.

I was left with no other option but to attempt, myself, to develop an entire theory of egg-boiling and then, alone, achieve a proper result, even if it meant the loss of a few eggs, which would need to be discarded.

I purchased an alcohol stove, five liters of alcohol, and a steam digester[1]—the use of which was familiar to

---

1. A type of early pressure cooker, developed in the 17th century

I Make Soft-Boiled Eggs

me from physics class during my secondary school years. Then I set to work. I poured water into the steam digester, placed ten eggs inside, and lit the alcohol stove.

After fifteen minutes, I removed the eggs from the steam digester. I cracked the shell off the first one—the egg was still hard. I repeated this with the second one—also hard. All the eggs were still hard. So I peeled the shells from all of the eggs and threw them once more into the steam digester. This time I boiled them for an hour. Still they remained dreadfully hard. And so I boiled them until morning. Despite my best efforts, they did not become soft.

In the morning, I was found sprawled over the basket of eggs. I had collapsed there in a state of despondency, having not managed to produce even a single soft-boiled egg. The eggs were as hard as ever.

1912

---

and used for the extraction of fat from bone.

Vodka of the Wood Vodka of the Strawberry:

Sketches from Galicia

No priest enjoys such enduring gratitude amongst his parishioners as does Father Plebań in Dąbrowice.

This fine old fellow will long be remembered in the entire region of Tarnów, and the descendants of today's parishioners will, in turn, recount to their children what they heard from their parents about this good man.

It was not his soulful sermons, which certainly bestowed satisfaction upon the souls of the good-natured farmers, nor even his piety that won him immortal renown in Dąbrowice, in its environs, and even in Tarnów. It was rather his green vodka, which he sometimes claimed enthusiastically to be the blood of his body, the essence of his mind, and the child of his intellect.

And the name of this product sounded scarcely less poetic: *Vodka of the Wood—Vodka of the Strawberry.*

He claimed to have given it this name sometime long ago. He had extracted the first little glassful after lengthy experimentation and sensed in the fresh green vodka the fragrance of all the forests surrounding Dąbrowice, the redolence of spring and summer, the scent of strawberry blossoms, and the taste of ripened strawberries. No one knew how the good priest manufactured this exceptional drink. It was only known that it was created chiefly from giant strawberries, which the priest collected in the forests with his own hands.

He always added an "Our Father" to his prayers, in the hope that there might blossom—in particular locations known only to him—an abundance of giant strawberries that he would himself gather in a giant basket.

Throughout August, light flickered all night long in the humble old parsonage. A pleasant aroma flowed out through the open windows, and when the children of the village climbed up the trees in the garden, they saw the long white hair of Father Plebań shimmering above curious snake-shaped apparatuses. They saw the priest, clutching a glass of his fresh product with a trembling hand, perform the sign of the cross piously, and slowly drink it down—heard him smack his lips and snap his fingers with such intensity that the cat, who purred contentedly behind the great oven, jumped up and took to its heels from the chamber with a snarl, as if someone had set a bundle of hay alight over its head.

In this moment, the priest seemed to them as if he were a supernatural being, and, in a state of holy reverence, the children climbed down from the priest's pear and apple trees, not neglecting to stash an ample amount of fruit in their shirts while doing so.

That was in August. November came and went amidst the filling of a great quantity of bottles and the adhering of labels, which the rector of Dąbrowice spent the entire winter designing and painting. On the labels, a fantastical St. Stanislaus blessed a little angel carrying a voluminous bottle, upon which an inscription was emblazoned in gold letters: *Vodka of the Wood—Vodka of the Strawberry.*

One Sunday, at that time of year when the first snows fell and wolves could be heard howling on the outskirts of the village, the priest announced, in a soft and emotional tone of voice, that he was inviting all the faithful to an afternoon hour of Catholic religious edification in the parsonage.

The spacious sitting room was full that Sunday, the parishioners packing themselves together tightly.

Father Plebań sat in an old, faded armchair, which had already served God knows how many priests, and, ever smiling, chatted pleasantly about the arrival of winter, and he urged them not to forget, on account of the cold, to visit the church and to be charitable towards the poor during

Advent season. To this, he added a few words about the approaching Christmas holiday and then disappeared from the chamber.

After some time, he returned with a basket full of bottles and distributed among his parishioners the green forest vodka—his strawberry vodka.

Tears filled the eyes of many as they looked upon his white head, his beloved visage, at how his chin trembled with pleasure as he presented them with his product. Their eyes grew moist at the thought of how it would be when the old priest dreamed his final, eternal dream under the birches and larches in the cemetery of Dąbrowice.

Thus arrived in Dąbrowice the winter that the good priest had so feared, and on account of which he had prayed to God all spring and summer, seeking forgiveness for the sins he had committed the previous winter, and which he would commit again in the coming one.

Occasionally he said to himself that this stockpiling of prayers was not entirely permissible, but he put his mind at ease with the thought that God already knew the weaknesses of humankind. And his winter transgression? It was the love of his green vodka.

On winter nights, he yearned for the green forests in which he loved to stroll. And so to transport himself back to the aromatic summer, he sat in the warmth of the great oven with a giant bottle of his own product.

Vodka of the Wood

As the first drops moistened his lips, there appeared before the priest's spiritual eyes the cool green of the oaks, birches, and spruces, and he saw before him the locations where the red of ripe strawberries gleamed.

The glass was quickly drained of its delicious green drink and had to be refilled routinely from the bottle beside it.

The breviary that he had laid out for himself remained unopened, and instead of the evening prayer, curious sounds were heard throughout the quiet chamber: the priest slurping extravagantly on the green, effervescent liquid.

The old priest sat, drank, and became lost in the thought of green forests—of spring and of summer—and it did not even disturb him that wolves howled in the vicinity of the parsonage and that gunshots, meant to disperse the hungry beasts, occasionally rang out.

Indeed, it also did not disturb him when his sister and caretaker, two years his junior, bewailed the sins of her brother and invoked all of the saints whose names occurred to her.

The priest said nothing. He just nodded his white head and continued to think of the fragrance of green forests.

When he repaired to bed, his head was usually spinning a bit, and he sang aloud a lengthy song of forest faeries and green vodka, causing his old sister to cover her ears.

Jaroslav Hašek

The next day, he would arise only shortly before noon and vow never again in his life to even so much as look at the diabolical drink. But what good was that?! Evening arrived, and the snow sparkled outside in the moonlight, and he was seized anew by a longing for summer and proceeded once more to down one glass after another.

Every day, over the course of many years, his sister prayed that the dear Lord might protect her brother from his infernal visions, but every winter such evenings occurred anew: the breviary sat undisturbed and the bottles emptied themselves. All for nothing was every pilgrimage to Kalwaria[1] and even to Częstochowa.[2] In vain were her donations of money there for a Holy Mass dedicated to her unfortunate brother.

When she thought about it, she cried bitterly. Every conceivable notion frightened her pious mind as she saw the priest suffer hellish torment. One winter, the devil—as she called it—led the priest into temptation with far greater success than usual.

---

1. A town in southern Poland noted for its extensive monastery, built during the Counter-Reformation. In the surrounding parkland, a series of 42 chapels recreates the path Jesus took to his crucifixion in Jerusalem.
2. The Jasna Góra Monastery in Częstochowa houses a Black Madonna, an icon in which the Virgin Mary and the infant Jesus are portrayed in black. This icon is the most popular pilgrimage destination in Poland and has been recognized by several pontiffs as worthy of special veneration.

Vodka of the Wood

On that occasion, before going to sleep, he sang his song of the forest faeries so loudly that Jurzik Owczyna—the municipal policeman, who was walking home late at night from the pub—stopped and stood before the parsonage. And after a while, a duet rang out in the still of the night.

One voice—rather powerful, yet dulled by the thick window glass—belonged to the priest, and the second, raspy one belonged to the municipal policeman. They must have sounded like wolves howling, since a group of farmers soon assembled with rifles and clubs in front of the parsonage. There, in a state of wonder and astonishment, they listened to Father Pleban's chant of forest faeries and green vodka, with such devotion as they might listen in church to litanies sung in honor of the Virgin Mary.

As the priest arose from his bed the next day, he learned from his tearful sister what a great commotion he had stirred up when the devil had tempted him on the evening prior.

He promised to change, but of course the nocturnal performance repeated itself, and half the village eaves-dropped dutifully beneath the window of his sleeping chamber, awestruck, mouths agape, as their aged pastor chanted curious elegies about green vodka and forest faeries.

Thenceforth, the song performances recurred with regularity, and the farmers turned up nightly to listen to the priest.

These were sad times for his sister. She saw hellfire everywhere she looked. It was then that she came to a decision and wrote a letter, with a trembling hand, to the consistorial vicar[3] of Tarnów. She begged that he might pay a visit, for the spiritual health of the priest of Dąbrowice, and speak to her brother with fatherly words, to free him from the snare and clutches of the devil. Without saying a word to her brother, she signed the page, moistened it with tears, and sent it to Tarnów.

Several days passed.

On one glorious winter's afternoon, a sled could be heard in front of the parsonage. Four fiery steeds stamped the frozen earth, kicking up dusty snow all around, and the esteemed consistorial vicar of Tarnów emerged and notified the bewildered priest that he had come to make his rounds.

The thought that someone in Tarnów might have learned something of his musical performances struck the priest like a bolt of lightning, and he dared not make eye contact with the gray-haired vicar, who was many years his junior, and who, for his own part, addressed the older, white-haired priest with the utmost respect.

---

3. An officer of the Catholic ecclesiastical court, in charge of adjudicating matters of church governance. The implication is that by asking for spiritual counsel the sister has also informed on her brother.

Vodka of the Wood

The esteemed lord vicar expressed his great satisfaction with the church, and after supper he sat across from the priest, seeking an opportunity, by one means or another, to satisfy the wishes of the sister, who remained in prayer in the adjacent room.

"This region is—no doubt—very lovely in the summertime," he began after a lengthy pause.

"Certainly, very lovely…", the priest confirmed wistfully, casting a furtive glance to the corner, where a giant bottle stood with its deliberately pious label.

"And there are forests here from which you must derive great pleasure in the summer," the vicar continued. "But in the winter, it is desolate, so one is best served by sitting in front of a warm oven and praying from the breviary. The contemplations of St. Augustine and the church fathers also make for beautiful reading. Every temptation of the devil will be frustrated thereby. Brother, I have brought with me several books on the eternal life and glorious contemplations of St. Augustine. It is best to read for two to three hours in the evening. I will go and fetch them."

With these words, he stepped into the adjacent room.

In that instant, the priest pulled himself together, sprang towards the bottle, and enjoyed a gulp of his wonderful drink.

When the esteemed vicar returned, a stack of books under his arm, the priest was once again sitting calmly in his place, gazing upward in a show of piety.

"This is a lecture that elevates the reader to another realm and casts out evil thoughts," said the lord vicar, laying the books down before the priest, and after some time, he added: "There is a fragrance here—it smells somehow like—like the forest."

"That is my *Vodka of the Wood—Vodka of the Strawberry*," the priest exclaimed joyfully and, without waiting for a response, filled two small glasses and raised a toast to the lord vicar.

They emptied the glasses.

"An exceptional taste, is it not?" inquired the priest, beaming, as he observed how the lord vicar licked his lips. "Another, no?" And they emptied the glasses once more.

"Exquisite, as if one were roaming through the forests in the summertime, taking in a breath of summer air," the visitor sighed longingly.

The eyes of the priest twinkled as he spoke of his product—the child of his intellect, the essence of his mind.

Both men sampled the green drink again and again, and before each new glass, the esteemed lord vicar whispered: "*Multum nocet—Multum nocet*,"[4] forgetting completely the purpose of his visit, the devil, St. Augustine, and the church fathers.

---

4. "Too much is harmful."

Vodka of the Wood

Then, when the farmers gathered together before the parsonage, as they did out of habit, they were astonished to hear, from the bed chamber of the priest, the song of the forest faeries and green vodka being sung no longer by one voice but rather by two; and the other, unfamiliar voice, was much more powerful.

Out of discretion, I will say no more but will add that this was hardly the last of the official visits, and when the esteemed lord vicar returned home to Tarnów on the third day and unpacked a giant bottle of *Vodka of the Wood—Vodka of the Strawberry*, he recognized, to his dismay, that several pages of St. Augustine and the church fathers had served as the wrapping for the bottle.

Vodka of the Wood—Vodka of the Strawberry had secured Father Plebań immortal renown in Dąbrowice.

1902

A Guest in the House
Is a God in the House

How admirable is the old Slavic saying, "a guest in the house is a god in the house," and how vast is the difference between East and West when it comes to hospitality.

If you are a guest in the East, you can walk about in your host's slippers, wearing nothing more than a dressing gown; if your host engages in relations with the maidservant, then he must stand by quietly during your stay, as you play first fiddle. You take precedence in all things: eating, drinking; if the horses are harnessed, take them to wherever you might desire. You may replace the staff, you may suggest renovations to the house. Should you be dissatisfied with the soup, then you may dump it on your host's head and dismiss the staff. In a nutshell: "A guest in the house is a god in the house."

In contrast, a guest among us in the West must show great deference to his host. He bows, kisses the hand of the lady of the house, eats everything on his plate with a forced smile—even if it's something his stomach does not tolerate—and obediently does anything that comes to the mind of his host.

And if you finally become fed up with this and protest, your host might very well banish you from the house.

Once you're gone, hundreds of bits of gossip arise in the city: that you chew tobacco; that you did not change your socks for a fortnight; that you never wipe your nose, and you use a table napkin if ever you do; that you borrowed 100 crowns from the maidservant; that you only came to be wined and dined; and that you courted the daughter of your host, despite you being married and already having eight children out of wedlock.

Every form of malicious gossip imaginable is directed at you: you are a furtive ne'er-do-well and desired nothing more than to eat your host out of house and home. Sadly there is sometimes an element of truth to this.

I have many a lovely memory of my visits to the Czech provinces. Apart from some minor fallout with the police on my return to Prague, I have only fond recollections of my noble deeds in the most far-flung reaches of the countryside.

Naturally, it's not so easy to establish oneself as a guest in any one place for too long a period.

Doing so demands a certain degree of impudent nonchalance, and one must act diplomatically and purposively. This is known as having common sense for living.

Consider, for instance, how lovely the autumnal season can be. Those who live in the big city know nothing of the magnificent views across the open countryside, which is drenched in the most sundry of hues. Forests and fields… but I beg your pardon, that's all silly, idle talk.

For me it is a matter of other things entirely. Autumn has still other beautiful offerings: goose, rabbit, partridge, and pheasant. Let the colorful foliage drop quietly upon trodden paths; we would much rather behold, for instance, the beauty of giblets. The gold of oaks and beeches may rain down in the forests; the autumnal copper of a wonderfully roasted goose is just as good, and has practical value to boot—a rabbit in cream sauce or with onions, the aroma of gravies from partridge, and the sweet fragrance of steamed chestnut stuffing in roast pheasant! All this is the bounty of the countryside in autumn. So who could not love the country, and who would not take pleasure in being in the midst of such splendor?

Now you need only find yourself a host! I discovered that all such game animals known for making the autumn so sublimely lovely can be found in abundance in the Bohemian-Moravian Highlands.

From among the various localities in this clime, I sought out a prosperous little town, where I felt convinced that someone could be found who would be capable of providing for me.

And so I turned up in the marketplace of that little town, amidst old historic houses, and began to proceed systematically. Above all I kept an eye out for businesses, and I found the sign "Karel Lábler, Wholesaler" to be the most satisfactory among them. This house was the largest of those on the square, and it made a very good impression.

I made for a nearby inn, where I struck up a conversation with the innkeeper: "Look at him, this Lábler, how well he is doing for himself these days. Back when he and my father..."

"What need is there to do well for oneself, coming from one of the town's oldest families, as he does? The family is estimated to have 200,000 crowns on hand, mister. His brother in Bousov is said to have just as much."

"Josef?"

"Yes, Josef." (I astonished even myself that I had guessed correctly on the first try.) "Josef Lábler—you know—the one who married the Hauser woman in Žďár. She was born in Chlum, then they relocated to Žďár, where they have a business. Her brother Jan shot himself dead during military maneuvers in Hungary."

I sighed: "Poor Jan, he looked so good in uniform, but he was an odd fellow. For example, to my mother he once remarked of me: 'Mr. Lábler will surely not have any recollection of him—perhaps he has never seen him before.'"

While the innkeeper stepped away, I wrote everything down, so as to keep my facts straight.

Karel Lábler
–Josef (brother), Bousov
–Hauser in Žďár (wife), previously of Chlum
–Jan (the brother, shot himself dead in Hungary)

When the innkeeper returned, I said "It really is a tragedy. You see, such is the nature of things in our entire family. My nephew on the other side of the family impaled himself on a fence at the age of five, and the cousin of my mother's aunt fell spontaneously through the floor into the cellar."

The innkeeper inquired if Mr. Lábler had yet been informed of my arrival. I waved my hand in a gesture of dismissal: "I don't know whether it would be agreeable to him. I am only a distant relative, after all, and don't like to impose."

"On the contrary, he'll be delighted—he's such a fine fellow, I'll have a girl sent for him."

After some time, a bespectacled older gentleman with a reddish face appeared at the inn. Brimming with delight, he approached my table.

He grasped my hand good-naturedly and began: "A member of the Lábler family, yes? From mother's side?"

Because every person comes from mother's side, I nodded my head and casually mentioned Josef from Bousov, the Hausers in Žďár—previously of Chlum—and Jan, who had gone bang during maneuvers in Hungary. I recall that we both cried for over five minutes.

Then it turned into a two-way sounding-out. I asked him how business was going with the coal. Here he corrected me, saying he had dealt only in grain and hay since long ago. I flattered him by saying that hay is a very important fodder, then spoke for over half an hour about various nonsense—whatever he liked. Then he asked me what I was actually hoping to accomplish here. Because nothing more clever occurred to me, I told him that I intended to write a book about the old cellars in this town because the Swedes[1] were alleged to have hidden out here. He seemed frightened by these Swedes, began to talk me out of it, then said that we could inspect his cellar tomorrow. It supposedly stretched all the way to the

---

1. A folk tradition originating with Sweden's invasion of the Holy Roman Empire (1630–1635) during the Thirty Years War. Under King Gustavus Adolphus, Sweden fought on the side of the Protestant forces against the Catholic-Habsburg coalition.

square where the courthouse was situated. Many cellars were said to be in the town, and I would undoubtedly be very pleased. There would be water in them here and there, so I would need to swim. However, I should not be concerned, as he would lend me a washtub.

I asked him which hotel he could recommend to me, and I could nearly have slapped myself across the face out of joy when he said "We have a whole slew of good hotels: *Moravec, Kubánkek, Zur Post,* and…"—I scarcely dared to breathe. I could have sunk into the earth— "… *Bei Budín, Beim Stelz,* but none of that is for you. You shall of course stay with me until you are finished with this cellar business. It is very important?"

"I mean to devote my entire life to it." We spoke for roughly another hour about cellars and cellar vaults. I explained to him that no one had taken notice of the cellars until now, even though they were deserving of it, and then we moved on to discussing caves and hunger towers.[2] The latter provoked our appetites, and so we went to lunch.

I began to lead a new life.

Suddenly I won favor throughout the entire town. After all, no person had ever before turned up wishing to

------

2. A series of round, fortified towers built in 1854 in the Swiss canton of Ticino, part of a defensive line against Austrian troops. The project employed the poor local peasantry of the area, and the fortifications became known as "hunger towers".

write a book about the cellars. The local superintendent of schools asked that I be introduced to him, and as I fulfilled his wish, he declared that he would be happy to assist me and that he had long taken an interest in the cellars of the town.

My host, Mr. Lábler, was enthused. He explained to everyone everything that he had learned from me. In a conversation with a local official, he explained that cellars are low, high, short, long, bright, dark, and wet.

I was invited into various homes to tour the cellars. I always arrived at approximately ten o'clock in the morning and declared that I would proceed with my cellar research after lunch.

As a matter of course I was invited to lunch in every one of these homes. After lunch, I would stretch out on the couch. And what lunches they were! Each luxuriated in the bounty of autumn, on which I have already remarked. Then, in the evenings, I would return to my host, who was already beginning, gradually, to lose his mind. At night, he walked about the house with a candle and crept into the cellar, where he sat on a ledge in a waterlogged corridor and shouted something or other into the darkness.

For the first week, he found it all to be in good fun, but, by the next week, he was already less amused, especially once I dropped certain hints and mentioned that I found this little town to be quite delightful and country living to be extraordinarily salubrious during the transitional period between autumn and winter—and that I would nevertheless be very pleased to return to Prague once the ice-skating season had begun.

He did not utter a word. He turned as white as a wall. Only after a while did he respond: "I understand." The good fellow was beginning to comprehend that his kitchen enticed me—that I felt quite at home with him.

In the early mornings, prior to the grocery shopping, I hurried to say "madam, today would be a very fine day to roast this-or-that—it would please me very much." At the close of the third week of my sojourn, the unfortunate Mr. Lábler began to make subtle insinuations concerning our familial ties. Eventually he resorted to direct speech: "Dear friend," he said with a wry grin, "whatever would we do if you were not my relative? I have been ruminating on various particulars, but I cannot seem to recall anyone of your name among our family."

"You're right about that," I replied calmly, "I, too, developed certain doubts once you began to tell me about your family. It seems to me that we are not related to each other in any way whatsoever. I'm actually rather pleased about this, because I can now show you far greater gratitude than I might have, had I been your relative. When one establishes oneself with relatives, one thinks that it is one's birthright to be catered to, and one feels very little sense of gratitude. An outsider, such as I, by contrast, feels the deepest sense of gratitude for the hospitality."

I continued to speak for a while, and I recall that we hugged and kissed one another. As we did so, I heard a sound reminiscent of the gnashing of teeth.

On this day, he traveled to the neighboring town, and we spoke no more. During his absence, I perceived a state of disorder in the residence and expressed the view that it would be best to reposition the furniture. Mrs. Lábler locked herself in her room and cried.

I find a gloomy environment disagreeable. I went outside and invited into the Lábler's home for cognac a posse of young people, whose acquaintance I had made over the course of my sojourn in the town. We drank up the entire supply.

Mrs. Lábler continued to cry.

The next morning, Mr. Lábler greeted me with a rifle. "Can you shoot?" he asked sweetly.

"No," I replied, because it seemed as if something malicious flared in his eyes.

"Well, it won't be so bad," he said, "you can learn with ease—we're going partridge hunting on my grounds."

"Then with the grace of God," I sighed, "hopefully nothing will befall me."

"If you handle the rifle with care, everything will go fine. You're certain you can't shoot?"

"Truly I cannot!"

He burst out laughing in such an unnatural manner that I could read it in his eyes: "This guest will certainly shoot himself dead in an unfortunate accident while on the hunt."

And so we went hunting.

At first, I didn't manage to shoot anything. He forced me to run repeatedly across a potato patch, taking care not to stumble. I acted as if I could not handle a rifle at all, and he shouted "Well, perhaps you will hit something, seeing as we have two flocks on the grounds." Suddenly I scared up a flock—boom!—four partridges fell to the ground. I fastened strings to their beaks, hung them on the back of my apron, and advanced briskly. He could not keep up, and so he shouted "Only to the stream, my grounds extend no further. This mountain is also a part of them."

He disappeared from my sight until evening. I brought down twenty partridges and carried the spoils into town; there I sold them to various inns. At one restaurant I explained that I sold them only out of necessity and hunger.

A guest in the house is a god in the house!

I returned to my host in good spirits and gave him his gun.

"What have you done with the partridges?"

"All twenty sold like hotcakes, a most hearty thanks," I said pacifically.

He turned pale, then let loose a frightful laugh and began to smash up the furniture. Of late his condition is improving. Yes, he continues to be kept under watch in the sanitarium, but he no longer rampages so. He looks about apathetically, and occasionally he smiles lethargically and whispers: "A guest in the house is a god in the house."

Only once in a while does he still roar: "Where is that fellow with my partridges?"

1912

The Story of a Respectable Person

Every evening, Mr. Havlik took stock of his activities for the day, to ascertain whether he had trespassed in any way against societal mores and public order, and whether he had fulfilled with proper thoroughness his obligations as a citizen, and as a member and parishioner of the Catholic Church.

And every evening, he could complete this accounting in the following manner: "I have found nothing that would result in my expulsion from respectable society." His chambermaid, an old lady, claimed that he was an eccentric, because every time he ventured out, he would say to her, in a good-natured tone: "Please, Mrs. Mlitschek, be so kind as to confirm that I've buttoned my trousers!"

It was precisely this that often plagued him and robbed him of peace. He felt ever more certain that a time was approaching when he would disgrace himself so thoroughly that he would become an abomination in the eyes of all honorable men. Whenever he crossed the street, he frequently stepped into a corridor so as to check his trousers; when he wore an overcoat or a winter jacket, he would warily unbutton it from time to time and check that everything was in order. Especially when he would walk into the wind, he had the strange, unnerving feeling that a heavy gust would unfasten all his buttons. But most embarrassing of all was when he found himself in female company, or sitting across from a young woman in a streetcar. On such occasions he would behave most nervously, constantly check the buttons of his jacket, and press his hands to his stomach, at which point his demeanor became so conspicuous that everyone looked at his trousers. Then he would perspire anxiously, flee the scene, and jump from the moving streetcar.

It was in just such a manner that he once broke a leg, lost consciousness, and came to in the entranceway of a building to which he had been carried, where a doctor had been summoned and was applying an emergency dressing in anticipation of the ambulance. With a weak voice, Mr. Havlik expressed the desire for a moment alone with the doctor. Once the onlookers had given them space, he whispered: "Doctor, I place my complete trust in you and ask you most sincerely, as a gentleman, to tell me whether I have buttoned my trousers properly." As a consequence, he was also treated for a concussion.

Only amid the boredom of the hospital did he have the opportunity to reflect on this matter, and, in a fevered state, he screamed unremittingly about something concerning trousers, leading others to believe that he was a tailor.

If he was very strict with himself, he was also strict when it came to the conduct of his fellow citizens, and he often found himself in difficult situations. In the restaurant where he dined for lunch, he noticed that the person adjacent to him was eating with a knife. He inquired what his neighbor did for a living and where he lived, and after he was filled in, learning that the neighbor was a senior legal secretary, Mr. Havlik dressed himself in a black suit that Sunday morning and paid the senior legal secretary a visit. He introduced himself and remarked cordially that he hoped the secretary would not be cross with him, but he had come with the most friendly intention of making him aware that, in the interest of propriety and social tact, he hoped he would not eat with a knife. The result was such that Mr. Havlik could write in his notebook: "November 29, between 10 and 11 o'clock, I was thrown down the stairs by Senior Legal Secretary Kehler, 8 Park Street, second floor."

As one might expect, in view of his primly modest lifestyle, he experienced many similar such encounters, making his diary ever more colorful. On one occasion, he was standing on the streetcar platform when a man, who was standing next to him, began to whistle a tune. Mr. Havlik observed this development with a feeling of unease, and when the whistling did not stop, he said: "Be so kind, good sir, as to think of social tact, and do not whistle."

The good fellow changed the tune and began to whistle: "Greenewill is off to war, he's marching through the Powder Tower."[1]

"Good sir," said Mr. Havlik, "think of your upbringing."

"If it doesn't suit you," came the answer, "then I will whistle 'A Stream Flows through Domažlice'. Do you enjoy songs of the Chodové?"[2]

"I see, to my dismay, sir," said Mr. Havlik softly, "that you are lacking in social tact."

"So you think me a lout?"

Had he not been so busy nodding his head, Mr. Havlik might have defended himself, but he nonetheless

---

1. The reference to Mr. Greenewill is obscure. The Powder Tower is a prominent landmark in Prague, a Gothic tower constructed in 1475 as one of the original city gates.
2. An ethnic group native to western Bohemia.

wrote in his diary: "March 12, between 5 and 6 o'clock in the evening, I was slapped from all sides during a ride through Hradčany. The public took the side of the perpetrator."

Pacing back and forth in his room with a swollen face, he said to his chambermaid: "Just look, Mrs. Mlitschek, is it not curious, the way that they battered me, because I admonished someone to behave respectably? Is it not an embarrassment, Mrs. Mlitschek?"

One day, Mr. Havlik went for a walk in Vinohrady, and it was there that catastrophe befell him. Directly in front of the town hall, a dog sat on the pavement. It sat there in such a manner as to make clear it had no respect whatsoever for the town hall of Vinohrady. Shortly thereafter, it departed, depositing on the walkway a roundish yellow mass, which demonstrated it was a relatively well-to-do dog that had feasted on bones for lunch.

For that reason, the citizens of Vinohrady took great pains to avoid the mass, and the constable stationed in the middle of the lane watched with great interest to see who would be the first to step in it. But the people stepped carefully around, and children leapt over it—until Mr. Havlik arrived.

He maintained a forward gaze because the writer of an editorial had once responded in the following manner to a question of his, regarding whether it was respectable to walk about with a sunken gaze:

Mr. V. H.

It is most indecorous to walk with a sunken gaze, for it gives the impression that one is looking for stray coins, which is a sign of avarice.

Thus he walked upright, and suddenly it was too late. He sensed that he had stepped in something soft, which had slipped away under his feet. He was startled and remained motionless. No, it could not be that he, an upstanding citizen, had stepped in such a thing. Perhaps it was an orange peel or a potato, he thought optimistically, and took a step forward to check.

But sure enough, it was precisely that which had immediately come to mind. Aghast, he went to the constable in the middle of the lane and said to him: "I beg your pardon most politely, have a look at what I've stepped in." In doing so, he turned around and raised his foot aloft so that the constable could see the calamity.

"It was a St. Bernard," said the constable.

"Certainly," said Mr. Havlik, "it is from a dog—be so polite as to tell me where I should lodge a complaint."

"It would be best if you went home and slept it off," said the constable, "don't bother me."

"But with your permission," objected Mr. Havlik, "I reckon it is your duty to look into the matter. Naturally, the owner of the dog must be punished."

"Go home," said the constable threateningly, "what are you thinking, speaking to a constable about excrement?"

"Please, I had no ill intention," stammered Mr. Havlik, "I only thought that it was a police matter to ensure that dogs do not soil the walkway. How is it that a tax-paying citizen could come to step in such a thing?"

People gathered all around, among them a stern fellow with a gray beard, in whom Mr. Havlik placed his confidence.

"Please," he said to him, "be so polite as to look at what I've stepped in, and when I made the constable aware of this, he regarded it as harassment of the police."

At this, the old gray man said to the constable: "Take him away!"

"At once, Lord Counselor!" said the constable, saluting as he grabbed Mr. Havlik by the collar.

When Mr. Havlik returned home, after having given notice of his identity, he was dreadfully pale and agitated.

"The police have come looking for you," Mrs. Mlitschek said insinuatingly.

"I know," he said, attempting a smile, and locked himself in his chambers. He placed his boots on the window sill, then went to the table, where he jotted down a few words on a sheet of paper. He then extinguished the oven flame, leaving the valve open so the gas could flow out, and lay down in bed. Before he lost consciousness, he repeated to himself what he had written down and bequeathed to the Czech public:

> I ask the Czech public to have a look at my boots, and they will come to know and comprehend everything. I ask for the forgiveness of the police for having stepped in it.

> Yours most respectfully,
> Wenzel Havlik.

1914

Successfully Saving the Suicidal:

A Sad Story

T hough no standing commission is maintained by the Prague City Council for the combating of suicide, tasked specifically with studying methods employed to that end in other major European cities, we can nonetheless point with pride to our municipal infrastructure for the rescue of persons attempting suicide by drowning.

This eminently sensible method consists of hanging life preservers attached to ropes, secured by lock and chain, at set intervals along the entire riverside. Small boxes, containing similar essentials for the rescue of persons attempting suicide by drowning, have also been built into the bridges of Prague. On these small boxes, as well as on the life preservers, a message is written: "For the saving of drowning persons. Misuse subject to punishment. Key in the care of the nearest patrolman." The idea for this fine provision originated with the Prague Committee for Housing Reform in the course of its travels through other major European cities. A very pleasing state of affairs, because if the commission can solve the suicide question, one can undoubtedly assume that they returned from their travels abroad with a plan for affordable housing.

It was announced that the city council would take part in a test of the life preservers, and I must say that the councilors demonstrated great mettle if they intended to persevere in the wind and rain, from eleven o'clock in the morning until eleven o'clock at night, just waiting along the bridges and riverside for some despairing person. However, no despairing person was to be found, and among the councilors none exhibited the resolve to leap from the bridge or riverside into the Vltava. As a result, the rescue infrastructure was securely shuttered, and the keys were consigned to the steering committee of the city council, where deliberations ensued concerning the proper course of action. Because the rescue equipment was sealed shut, some questioned why it had been installed in the first place. A clamor arose in favor of establishing a special administration for this matter of tremendous gravity; it was proposed that the office of "Highest Municipal

Rescuer" be created, to whom five officials with the simple title of "Municipal Rescuer" and several paid apprentices with the title of "Aspirant to the Municipal Rescue Administration" would be subordinated.

Ominous clouds gathered concerning the fates of the suicidal, as the city council appeared to be proceeding with true pomp and circumstance. Any who wished not to squander this favorable opportunity thus leapt into the water posthaste. And so it happened that some thirty men and women drowned in the course of those momentous deliberations over the keys. Fortunately for them, the city council was at loggerheads in their efforts to fill the prospective office, since one member had a cousin, another an uncle, this one a nephew and another a son, and so on. Thus the office remained unoccupied, so as not to expose the nepotism that prevailed at city hall.

A special task force was established to plan out the systematic distribution of the keys to the life preservers and ropes. The task force undertook the work with great enthusiasm, and they did a glorious job of it, as the message on the boxes for the rescue of drowning persons, closed under lock and key, attests: "For the saving of drowning persons. Misuse subject to punishment. Key in the care of the nearest patrolman."

Before the keys were distributed to the police, another trial run was held, and the members of the city council had the good fortune to see a tailor leap from the Charles

Bridge into the Vltava before their very eyes. They quickly threw him a secured life preserver, but the heroic tailor declined to take hold of it and vanished, in a fit of cursing, beneath the river's surface. For this reason, the city council had a polite request to the suicidal inscribed on the life preservers: "Please grab hold of the life preserver!" After this auspicious trial run, the police received the keys, which they, in turn, entrusted to the individual commissioners' offices. The latter delivered them to the watchmen, who patrolled along the river, with instruction that whosoever found themselves nearest to such an incident must take action.

As anyone can appreciate, this arrangement is extraordinarily appropriate and practical because, as one can see from the case I shall describe, the life preserver underwent scarcely any wear, the lock was not damaged, the rope did not get wet, and thus, unlike Prague's cobbled pavement, constant repair and replacement was not necessary. The case that I shall mention here is very tragic, and I beseech the reader to read these lines, which I dedicate to my poor, distraught Aunt Sophie, with the necessary respect.

She was already an elderly soul, but her love of animals endowed her with the sort of infinite grace that makes such ladies so congenial. Some keep dogs, cats, or birds at home, but my poor aunt kept salamanders. She had eight of them in total and cared for them with that remarkably tender care of which only such elderly, sensitive souls are capable. Yet human happiness rarely endures. The same goes for salamanders. If one loses a family member, the loss is painful. But what a blow for my aunt when all eight salamanders croaked at once!

From that moment forth, I did not part from her side. I wished to compensate for the loss of the salamanders through filial love. Sadly, it was in vain. My poor aunt saw in me only her nephew—not a salamander tumbling about merrily in the water. She grew melancholy, and only when I climbed into a giant tub before her eyes and floundered about there did she take me for a salamander and forget her grief for a moment. And once, when I painted myself black and yellow, she appeared to be cured of her dejection.

After a short time, however, her pain resurfaced anew, and her only desire was to stroll with me along the riverside. The water reminded her of her darlings, and it beckoned her too! Alas! One day, we found ourselves again at the river and were walking over the Charles Bridge. She was despondent throughout the entire stroll, and as we reached the cross in the middle of the bridge, she asked me:

"Is it deep here?"

"Quite so, dear aunt."

"And if I were to jump down from here, would I drown?"

"Most certainly, dear aunt."

For a time, she grew silent, only after a while remarking: "Did you know that I was a circus performer as a young girl?"

At that the old lady vaulted over the bridge wall—just like the great jumpers of the Olympic Games—and plummeted into the water below.

There was a gurgling, then she swam downstream, and I went flying to the nearest patrolman to procure the key to the sealed box with the life preserver and rope.

I found him at the Church of the Knights of the Cross. He was observing the pigeons on the roof there.

I explained to him what had happened. He pulled out his notebook: "So you are saying that it was your aunt. Are you certain?"

"I can confirm it."

"Good, and so you want the key to the rescue articles. And do you know from what location she jumped into the water?"

"Next to the statue of St. John of Nepomuk, she was always a great votary of his."

"Yes, my dear sir, then nothing can be done from here. I cannot give you the key because I am not the most proximate patrolman. In this case, the nearest is the patrolman at the Bridge Gate. Go and get the key from him, but swiftly—it is a matter of a human life!"

I ran and found the patrolman in the Bridge Lane, a good distance beyond the Bridge Gate.

Saving the Suicidal

"My good sir, I am not the nearest. If my colleague is presently by the Church of the Knights of the Cross, then he is in fact the nearest. Run to him!"

I ran back to him, but he was already in the Charles Alley, behind the Clementinum.[1]

He laughed, because, once again, he was not the nearest: "That is a vexatious thing, now the patrolman in Bridge Lane is the nearest. Let us hope that your aunt does not drown before you reach him!"

His fears were realized. She drowned as I conversed with him in the Charles Alley; however, I do believe that he was the nearest, since the other patrolman had reached the inner ring road in the meantime.[2]

1912

---

1. A complex of historic buildings in central Prague, housing, among other landmarks, the National Library of the Czech Republic.
2. The length of the Charles Bridge (500 meters or 1600 feet) contributes to the dark hyperbole of this piece. The narrator would have had to run at least a half a kilometer between the various Prague landmarks to save his poor aunt.

A Legitimate Business

Once upon a time, I sat on a bench in the park at Charles Square with the dearly departed Mestek.

Mestek, then the proprietor of a flea circus, was in a very despondent mood, for he had come to the realization that fleas were no longer suited for the purposes of training. A catastrophe had recently befallen his circus. Some drunken fellow, driven by the crazed conviction that the entire thing was a sham, had entered his booth and—without even so much as attempting to verify his assumption—struck with his cane the carton containing the circus. The trained fleas were delivered in this way from the yoke of their microscopically small paper carts, winning their freedom. Even the peep show with the magnifying glass was demolished. On the floor of the carton remained sprawled the corpse of a little flea man—a virtuoso who had been the soul of the circus. Mestek had referred to him endearingly as "Little František". The corpse of the artist was identified under the magnifying glass; he could be recognized only because he was missing a leg.

It numbered among the secrets of such circuses that a leg was removed from the performers, so they would not jump around in too unruly a manner and disturb the ceremonious procession.

Only one flea, with broken legs and an overturned little cart, had endured amongst the dead. "I thought," Mestek said with a sigh, "that I could revive her, but my efforts were in vain. Our Pepina languished, so finally I squashed her."

Mestek spoke for a while of the love between Pepina and Little František and of how the tiny flea dame had gazed adoringly upon the tiny flea gent while he danced.

"Never again in my life will I ever meet so clever a creature," Mestek said. "The fleas of today have fallen into degeneracy. They are not what they once were. They've become dimwitted. Perhaps a new species of flea is upon us. I recently purchased a full bottle of fleas from the custodian of the old town asylum, but not one of them was worth a thing. I had fleas from the police station, from various orphanages; fleas from the boarding school they call '*Happy Home*', from Eliška Krásnohorská's boarding school, fleas from the penitentiaries, from the barracks, from the pawnshops, fleas from several hotels, from the Karolinum and Clementinum building complexes, fleas from the girls' finishing school and from the manufacturers' association, from the Emmaus Monastery and from elsewhere, and all of these fleas were entirely incompetent. Of course, I found two or three that one might have described as talented, but they were devoid of any ambition. The career did not entice them. They ran off without considering what grand and illustrious fame awaited them. The new, younger generation of fleas will never boast of a Pepina or a Little František. Their quality cannot be articulated in plain language—only in silence can we honor and pay homage to them..."

We were overcome by a sense of melancholy as we relived in our minds the triumphal procession of the flea circus through Bohemia, Moravia, and—on one brief tour—through Hungary, where the Hungarian gendarmes escorted us back to the border, since they regarded our flea circus as a covert form of pan-Slavic propaganda.

In some parts of Moravia, we were obstructed by the clergy.

As I familiarized the priest of Helštýn with the concept of our circus, he explained to me: "I could not suggest your enterprise to the faithful of my parish, for it cannot endear them to God. The training of fleas is in contradiction with the nature of man. As told to us by Abbot Anselmus, the fleas of the Middle Ages induced the monks of the monasteries—through incessant biting that prevented them from getting any rest—to appeal to God day and night."

"So you regard fleas as sacred creatures?" I asked. "Then I can assure you that we have fleas in our circus descended from those who once bedeviled the baby Jesus in the manger at Bethlehem."

At this, he turned violent, so I knocked him out cold, but in the end we were forced to retreat to the mountains with the flea circus, for the priest had incited the entire region as far as Walachia against us.

Mestek interrupted our spell of contemplative brooding: "If one is patient and enterprising, he will triumph over the stupidity of mankind. One need only go about things in a clever manner. It doesn't matter if one paints a duck; what matters is convincing the spectator that it's not a duck but rather a jaguar. Should that business prove unsuccessful, a second or a third such business will undoubtedly succeed."

"Human beings are jackasses," he said, elaborating on his philosophy. "The greater the nonsense, the more people will dig into their pockets to witness it. The people are in need of new astonishments. What do you think?"

A Legitimate Business

"I am of the view," I replied, "that there are very few free-thinking people. Those with definite, idiosyncratic views don't usually come to us. Our performances are always attended by audiences convinced they will see all that we have advertised, and that it will all be worth seeing. Recall the bat we captured at Bohdalec, on the outskirts of Prague, that we promoted as a flying lizard from Australia! And everyone paid the requested sum to behold it. Or think back on how people fought for tickets to see the offspring of the king snake that strangled the English viceroy of India? Yet it was just a baby grass snake. And do you remember how many people were in attendance when Pepíček Vanek from Košíre pretended to be an orangutan from the island of Borneo?"

"What a swindler," Mestek responded. "How could I forget? Before the final performance, he demanded twenty crowns from us because he thought fifteen plus meals was insufficient for playing the part of an orangutan. And besides, the fellow earned a pretty penny from the fruit and other goodies people threw into his cage. He always stashed that stuff in the corner, selling it to the peddler woman across the street when we closed the booth for the evening. So I refused to pay him more. That caused him to go ape, and, in the middle of a performance, he began to sing "On Radlitzer Street" as an orangutan. And what a panic it caused! Then we were thrown out of Tábor. We had far more success with the mummy of the English King Richard III, notwithstanding that the mummy was nothing more than a bundle of ram's hide. Only after half a year had passed were we found out. You spoke brilliantly in front of that ram's hide: 'Here you shall see a representation of the greatest and most terrible monstrosity that ever sat upon a royal throne. This royal villain, whom a degeneration of the body transformed into a monster and an ogre, who waded in the blood of countless misdeeds and astonished even Shakespeare with his perfidious thirst for blood, this royal ogre has dried up, and we are very pleased to present him to you, the esteemed public, in the form of a mummy—a husk…'"

"Then a district official confiscated Richard III," I added.

"However, from this one may deduce," Mestek philosophized further, "that everything is possible in this world. I would bet that more than half the Earth's population earns a living from one form of fraud or another. Now it's only a matter of us thinking up something new to present to the audience. One must inspire a bit of wonder in them. It should make such an impression that all those taken in will spread the word for us. We will show them something."

"Hang on a minute with the 'show them *something*'," I interrupted, drawing with my walking stick in the sand. "Why this '*something*'? Let's go one step further. Do you get me? Show the audience *nothing*!"

A Legitimate Business

"At least a pebble," pled Mestek, "I have always shown *something.*"

"Not even so much as a pebble," I maintained, "*something* is rubbish—old school. I tell you that we shall show the audience *nothing at all.* And that is precisely the surprise. You say: 'at least a pebble', as was often done in the past. One says: 'This pebble is from Mars.' The audience members go home with the impression that they have seen something and were not surprised. But when the audience sees absolutely nothing at all, then they will be completely astonished. Just look!"

I sketched in the sand with my walking stick. "Our booth will be round, spacious, windowless, and without any opening in the ceiling. It must be completely dark. Two doorways will be covered with curtains: through one, in the front, the audience will enter, and the other will serve as an exit. That one is in the rear. A giant sign: 'The greatest surprise in the world! A surprise you will never forget. Admission for adult males only. Women and children not permitted. Half-price admission for soldiers!' The audience will be admitted individually at short intervals. I will stand outside, serving as the promoter and cashier. You're in the dark booth, and, as soon as someone turns up, you grab them by the trousers and shirt collar and throw them back out through the rear exit, without a word. A small, modest entrance fee, and you'll see—no one will regret it. I assure you that people only desire the worst for one another, that they will even publicize it and encourage others to have a look. A giant surprise, a marvelous thing. Our business will be built on a foundation of psychology."

Mestek dithered for a while, not because he had a principled objection to this new enterprise of amusement, but only on account of wanting to bring it to perfection.

"Would it not be good," he submitted for consideration, after some deliberation, "to strike each person with a cane in the process? That would make the surprise all the greater."

I was decidedly against this. "We would only delay ourselves thereby. The entire procedure must unfold as quickly as possible. One enters the darkness and is suddenly back outside. He shall scarcely have enough time to get his bearings. Therein resides the truly authentic surprise. The business is completely legitimate! We promise nothing which we cannot deliver. We promise a surprise, and we keep our word. No one may accuse us of being scammers."

Our legitimate business enjoyed enormous interest. We first pitched our tent in Benešov, where all the optimal conditions were to be found: the military and an inquisitive audience. I had placards printed that matched the sign on our booth:

A Legitimate Business

! Titillating !
! Only for adult males !
! Huge surprise !
! Our establishment is one you'll never forget !
! No nonsense—satisfaction guaranteed !

The placards, the reasonable 20-heller admission fee, and the enigma of a piquant and mysterious surprise for adult males attracted a vast host of men—soldiers and civilians—to our booth.

In the crowd could be seen sixteen-year-old lads who were ready to tell me they were forty or fifty just to be admitted.

We began at six o'clock. The first patron was a husky man who had been waiting since five o'clock and flew fast as lightning through our booth, ending up back in the fresh air on the other side.

I listened as he remarked to the audience: "That's phenomenal; you must have a look at it too."

I was not mistaken concerning the psychology of the masses. Those whom we tossed out did much for our publicity. Within an hour and a half, a few hundred adult men passed through the muscular arms of Mestek. Some even had themselves thrown out two or three times, returning to the booth and falling once more into Mestek's powerful hands. Every face shone with delight and satisfaction. I observed that many of them brought along acquaintances, wholeheartedly extolling the "huge surprise."

Where the devil can't go himself, he sends a district official. One arrived shortly after half-past seven. "Do you have a license?" he asked me at the entrance. "Please go right in," I replied. A brief struggle broke out between him and Mestek in the darkness of the booth. The official, conscious of the dignity of his office, defended himself desperately against the big surprise, but, in the end, he too went flying out the rear exit into the jubilant crowd.

Then the gendarmes arrived, shut down our booth, and hauled us off to court, on account of affronting a local official and resisting arrest.

"For the rest of my days I shall never again establish a legitimate business," Mestek assured me, as we made ourselves at home on our plank bed. "From this day forth, I shall live by fraud alone."

1921

The Beckov Monastery

Some four years ago, I became acquainted with the friars of Beckov Monastery. They were jovial Franciscans, and I wish to recount what it was like to be in their company.

I arrived at Beckov via the Váh River, for the purpose of searching, among the locals, for traces of the Kipchak peoples.[1] It is unnecessary to go further into these particular details; mostly I used this as a pretense to gain admission to the monastery by means of subterfuge—in short, to dupe the venerable abbot.

---

1. The Kipchaks were a Turkic nomadic group that inhabited the Eurasian Steppe during Middle Ages. With the Cumans, another Turkic people, they formed the Cuman–Kipchak Confederation which ruled much of Central Asia from the 11th to the 13th century, their territory extending as far west as the Danube.

I knocked on the monastery gate and presented my visitor's card, on which was written "Your Reverence, I turn to you for the sake of research on the Kipchaks, whose traces I seek in the Váh River Valley." Below this was stated simply "I request accommodations and permission to conduct research in the monastery archive." The father who had admitted me escorted me at once through the cloister, to inform Abbot Eusebius of my arrival.

After some time, Abbot Eusebius appeared. He shook my hand, admitting with embarrassment that he knew nothing of the Kipchaks. *So he was equally as knowledgeable as I!* As far as the archive was concerned, he told me it stood at my disposal, and I could stay at the monastery for so long as I might desire. He then led me into the refectory, where the friars sat playing chess.

He introduced me to them, and Father Liberatus showed me to my room, from which one had a marvelous view of the Váh River. He opened the window and pointed to the surrounding landscape: "All of this is ours!" Far and wide there were fertile fields in which golden grain glistened. The verdant meadows, the blue forests, all of it belonged to the Franciscans of Beckov!

As he spoke with me about the blessings of God, ecstasy was plainly discernible in his eyes—and in the fat of his cheeks.

Inviting me into his chamber, where the fragrance of roses and basil wafted through the windows, he removed from a cabinet a can of sardines that he opened and offered to me, as he produced, from another cabinet, a bottle of cognac.

We then drank, smoked cigars, and discussed all sorts of things: flooding, which people feared needlessly, because it was averted by means of fervent prayer; the merciful summer; the harvest; how God Almighty saw to the prosperity of the crops; the bountiful yield of hay; and the beauty of clover.

He led me up the tower of the monastery and, pointing to a cluster of buildings below, said that what I beheld was the monastery homestead, which housed some four hundred cows and three hundred pigs, and they had a chicken farm besides. Farther in the distance was to be found a sheep farm with four hundred sheep and, farther still, towards the forest, a fenced enclosure for the rearing of pheasants. In the surrounding forests worked eight gamekeepers and two woodsmen. There was game in abundance: big game, roe deer and fallow deer, rabbit, partridge, and wild boar.

As he described this all to me in vivid detail, the dear Father Liberatus folded his hands humbly and exclaimed: "God is gracious!"

Meanwhile, we were already being sought after; dinnertime had arrived.

The twelve of us sat around a long table, and as we arose and said a brief prayer—that God might be so gracious as to grant us a good appetite—the friars proceeded to dole out steaming dishes.

The dignified monastery cuisine! God, the Almighty, had conferred a providential hand upon the brother chef of the Beckov Monastery, and in his endless benevolence, he bestowed upon us a chicken soup with finely chopped chicken innards and chicken breast, a glass of Madeira wine and—shortly thereafter—pheasant stuffed with chestnuts.

The mercy of God was proven further still upon the serving of roast gosling with salad.

Raw delight shone in the eyes of the friars, and before the baked trout was served, we thanked the dear Lord once more for a short interval. The trout tasted exquisite. We comprehended the benevolence of God, who had created all these magnificent things so the Franciscans might fare well upon the Earth.

God had also created wine. And what wine they had at the Beckov Monastery!

It was so splendid and superb a wine that one could not drink enough of it, and the glasses had to be refilled continuously.

The hours passed in a state of convivial fellowship. We smoked cigars, and the Abbot told lovely stories.

The friars spoke one after another. Soon Father Fortunatus took the floor, then once again Father Liberatus, and they began to tell unseemly tales, which they took care to introduce in the following manner: "It is hard to believe how profligate the world is nowadays. As I rode to a feast at the monastery in Trenčín, a coachman recounted to me a lewd story that some man had told to him. I do not exaggerate in saying that the scoundrel committed sin with his words, as the following story demonstrates."

And so the story was told. Much was only insinuated through gestures. Then we were offered the finest cognac. The sun was already rising over Trenčín.

Confound it! I felt no desire to sleep. As the lord fathers retired to their chambers, I stepped out of the monastery and strolled through the fields.

The workday was already in full swing in the meadows. Amid the gray dawn, grass was being reaped for the monastery's cows. At the edge of the forest, a little old man was sharpening a scythe. "God's blessings!" he said.

"How fare ye?" I asked in response.

"In truth, I mean not to commit sin, but how well can I fare, really?" the old man replied.

"How well can I fare?" he repeated, in a melancholy tone, "I work all day long for the gracious lords of the monastery, and they pay only twelve kreuzer per day, with no rations, because they must be frugal for the Pope."

With this, he made the sign of the cross and continued to sharpen his scythe in the still of the morning, as a mist dispersed gently over the Váh and twelve Franciscan friars lay snoring in the Beckov Monastery.

1909

The Rescue Mission

Not so long ago, controversy erupted between Galicia and Hungary over Morskie Oko.[1] Actually, it was more about the ferry that floated upon this lake, from which tourists threw stones into the greenish water, since it no longer served a sensible purpose. One day, a great storm came and unfastened the ferry from its anchor, and lumberjacks in the employ of the Hungarian Forestry Administration secured it. Lumberjacks of the Galician Forestry Administration observed this from the opposing lakeshore and reported

1. A lake on the border of present-day Poland and Slovakia, in the Tatra Mountains, a northern extension of the Carpathian mountain range.

the entire matter to officials in Nowy Targ. After that, Galician gendarmes pulled the ferry to their side and declared that it belonged to them. The Hungarian authorities relayed the report onward, to Pest, whereupon the Hungarian Minister of Interior transmitted a note of protest to Vienna and asserted that this tiny lake in the heights of the Tatra Mountains, as well as the ferry, belonged to the Hungarian crown. However, from the governor's palace in Lviv, it was asserted that Morskie Oko belonged to Galicia and so too did the ferry. In the meantime, this hotly contested ferry was stolen by shepherds, who used the wood to mend their dilapidated huts on the mountainside.

It was now a matter of the entire lake!

At the water's edge stands a tourist cabin. One day, Hungarian gendarmes arrived and sealed the cabin shut from the Hungarian side. A few days later, Galician gendarmes came and sealed the cabin from the Galician side, and it very nearly came to a shootout with the Hungarians.

The situation was very tense. The Hungarians shouted: "Morskie Oko belongs to Hungary!" and the Galicians: "Morskie Oko belongs to Galicia!"

In this way, it came to blows between the citizens of the two lands, and on the way home, both sang their national anthems.

Such was the nature of their relations when I scaled the cliffs overlooking Morskie Oko with a friend.

Rescue Mission

On one side of the ravine leered the Hungarians, and on the other side leered the Galicians.

Suddenly, my friend lost his balance, cried "I'm falling!" and proceeded to plummet, from a height of eighty meters, down into the depths, landing in a thicket of dwarf pines.

He had fallen to the Galician side, from which one must hike around the Tatra Mountains in their entirety before one arrives at a Galician village where any sort of assistance could be expected.

Thus it was only natural that I sought help on the Hungarian side.

I descended from the cliffs and arrived at a cottage. Here I encountered an old shepherd smoking a short pipe, surrounded by pasturing sheep. In response to my greeting, he yawned and said nothing. I reported the fall to him, to which he smilingly opined: "He has thus fallen by the will of God, the wolves shall tear him to pieces in the brush."

"Surely an effort must be made to help him," I replied. He shrugged his shoulders.

"The wolves are devouring him, and if he runs into a bear, then he's surely finished. I beg you most humbly for some money for a bit of tobacco. I shall pray for the departed."

I gave the thoughtful man money for tobacco and ran farther down the mountain.

The next place where I could expect to find help was in Spiš.

It was late at night by the time I arrived there.

A dozing watchman sat on a platform at the gendarmerie. Once I had explained everything to him, he spat and said: "*Isten biszony*, God as my witness, I can be of no assistance in this matter. You must wait until tomorrow morning, when the cavalry captain arrives. But tread carefully and say nothing suspicious, because our lord cavalry captain is an odd fellow. He might convince you he has no time and then say to me 'Let the man wait until I return,' mount his horse and ride to Lviv, where he will proceed to drink for a week; in this case, I would be required to hold you captive until he returns and deals with you, throws you out, or has you locked up. He is otherwise a fine person, just an odd fellow. Of course, it could also happen that he puts you in a wagon, takes you to Lviv with him, and has gypsies perform for you. In that case, you would have to sing and drink with him until he has you arrested in Košice."

I thanked him for the information and waited in the train station until morning, since all the hotels were already closed. In the morning, I sought the cavalry captain. He was in a good mood that day and laughed heartily as I explained that my friend had fallen from the cliffs overlooking the Lomnica Forest. "So he has fallen, that's good. Haste is needed in this matter. I shall have a rescue expedition assembled immediately." To the watchman, he commanded "Bring the map." He opened it and said to me "Here is the Lomnica Forest, right?"

"Yes, and here, from the Hungarian side, is where we ascended. My friend lost his balance up there and fell northward."

The cavalry captain had barely heard my story when he slammed his fist on the table and grumbled: "Northward, you say? The impudence! You climb up from Hungary, and he—this lout—falls in the direction of Galicia, towards that dastardly Galicia? Scandal! This is an affront! If he climbed up from the Hungarian side, he should have fallen to the Hungarian side—not the Polish one. Get lost! The Galician authorities should take care of you. Surely your friend did this intentionally."

I took a wagon and rode along the Klotylde trail and arrived very late in the evening, thoroughly exhausted, at Zakopane, on the Polish side.

The Polish gendarmes received me very politely.

That was quite a difference.

"The most rapid help is necessary in this matter, without any question," reckoned the gendarme obligingly, "we have not a moment to lose and must report to Nowy Targ immediately. We must go at once to the head gendarmerie watchman of the highest security office."

Thus we made for Nowy Targ and arrived in the morning hours. There too, I found only attentive people. "Naturally, rapid help," it was said to me, "act quickly and prudently. First, we must go to Myślenice. The rescue station there is responsible for mishaps in the Tatra Mountains. We must mobilize rescue teams there as quickly as possible, to reach the site of the accident."

We traveled twenty kilometers farther from the site of the accident.

We were received in Myślenice with the utmost courtesy. A day and a half had passed by the time we had drummed up all the members of the rescue station, but we did have courageous and determined people. How quickly they rustled up the maps and ropes! One of them even brought along four hatchets. From this rescue troop one might have easily gotten the impression that we were going to kill my unfortunate friend.

The trip to Nowy Targ had gone quickly; in the meantime, four days had passed since the mishap. We stopped at the gendarmerie watch station in a podunk town.

"Friends," said the head watchman of the gendarmerie, "we have under lock and key the man who fell from the cliffs overlooking Lomnica. He fell into the protected pine woods and was picked up there by a patrol. He broke eight trees in the fall, so we arrested him."

At this news, the rescue team dispersed without a word.

1911

Money Troubles

After fifteen years, the aged Šíma, clerk at the Procházka & Co. Banking House, had worked up the courage to knock on the office door of financier Procházka and request a salary increase of twenty crowns for the new fiscal year.

Šíma now sat down before Mr. Procházka, who had asked him to do so upon hearing his request. Pacing back and forth in his office, his boss gesticulated excitedly as he lectured: "I could have you thrown right out of here with your obscene request, but, seeing as I happen to have half an hour to spare, I wish to speak with you, as one might with a friend. You would like me to raise your salary by twenty crowns monthly—thus by 240 crowns per year. And you desire this from me at a time when a downturn hangs over the financial market like a sword of Damocles? Are you aware that Alpine securities have declined from 772 to 759.60, that shares of the Friedrich Works have fallen from 940 to 938? The stock price of arms manufacturers is sinking as well, my dear Mr. Šíma. From 728 to 716.40! That is horrendous. And you want a bonus of twenty crowns!"

He wrung his hands and exclaimed: "Bank shares are unstable. The leading securities, shares of the Austrian Credit Association, have weakened in recent days—a drop of five crowns to 664.90—and you desire a twenty-crown pay increase! Trading at current market value makes for depressed and lousy transactions, shares of the state railway have fallen by an entire twelve crowns, the Italian government cannot acquire a loan of even 100 million crowns from France, but you seek from me a twenty-crown bonus! France attempts to sell off its steelworks, the sale of Russian crownland is rumored, and you come to me and say, as if it were all so self-evident: 'I have served loyally for fifteen years, boss, and now I take the liberty of requesting—bearing in mind financial hardship, general inflation, my ten children, my hole-riddled shoes, and my infirmity—a monthly pay increase of twenty crowns.' You are correct, hapless fellow, the financial hardship is grievous. Shares of the Southern Railway have fallen by five crowns, and I hold them in large quantities… but why do I bother explaining that to you, my dear man?! Notice that today even the fortunes of the Buschtěhrader Railway have declined: on one index shares of the Buschtěhrader Railway have fallen from 2515 to 2426 and, on another, from 1004 to 976. You are certifiably insane with your demand for a salary increase! It is pure madness, my dear man! Just pay a visit to the Prague Exchange! So much rests on the market, comprised of quotes of this kind! But what good is any of it?! The stocks exhibit ominous fluctuation. Not a single one remains steady. Shares of the Credit Bank, which once traded at 760, have fallen to 750.75. What do you say to that? Do you still want a bonus, my dear old man? Do you remain adamant in your request, which fails to consider that the Swiss government could scarcely rustle up the two million that they require for circulation? Yes indeed, my dear old man! The monthly balance sheets for the sale of gold are not favorable. The balance sheets for this fiscal year are enough to make one go mad. Romania, Turkey, Bulgaria, and Greece are practically insolvent, and you desire that I raise your wages! Spain, Portugal, and Italy cannot find debt relief anywhere. The banking house Français Fréres in Lyon has suffered a loss of 150 million in an expedition to Morocco, and you come to me calmly and spout off: 'Boss, I ask for a raise of twenty crowns.' My dear man, have you any idea that a merger between the Rositzer

Mines and the Friedrich Works is under discussion, and do you know that the acquisition of mining shares in the Anna Maria Mines would lead to a decrease of twenty thousand crowns in annual revenue? Nowhere is speculation favorable. Just try and buy shares of the Podoler Cement Manufactory, my dear old man, and see how much swagger you will have then; just try your hand at the stock market! You shake your head, so it seems you won't! You might think that at least shares of the Koliner Chemical Fertilizer Plant remain steady at 379. I acquired them at 382, so I lose three crowns. Believe me, my dear man, when I say I can't even bare to look at you! You sit there like a log! May the devil take you, along with all the stocks in the sugar industry. I tell you that these too fare poorly, and you get no more than 261.50 if you squeeze them for all that they're worth. No one would dare offer them to me, much less the stock of the Doctor Kolben Factory—that much I know for certain. I would set that person straight, my dear old man! Do you know that the Wienerberger Brickworks Association stands at the brink of ruin, and that the American billionaire Brown has shot himself? Do you know that the financiers Müller, Skabat, Kovner, and Hübner took their own lives, that the bankers Mains, Quinay, Rêche, and Bulechard hanged themselves? Do you know that the investors Commot, Karelt, and Morrisson and the banker Hammerles and his partner have jumped into rivers, canals, and seas? Do you know that there's one bankruptcy after the next, that the coal pits are burning in Alaska, and an American coal baron has cast himself into the flames? Do you know that the sulfur mines in the Ural Mountains were destroyed by an earthquake, that the Oldenburger fortune has halved in value, that the Salzburg Railroad and Tramway Corporation has gone under? Surely you were not aware of that, otherwise you would not demand from me a monthly salary increase of twenty crowns…"

The financier Procházka shook the motionless Šíma, who fell from his chair, limbs frozen.

The sheer scale of financial misery had caused him to die of a broken heart.

1910

The Reform Efforts of Baron Kleinhampl

Baron Kleinhampl was a very wise man, and once he inherited the manor at Bítouchov from his aunt, he contemplated day and night how he might usefully renovate his newly acquired estate.

He found first and foremost that the mighty old oak trees in the park deprived his manor of a view, and so he had the caretaker of his new property summoned and gave him the order to transplant these behemoths elsewhere.

The caretaker milled about agitatedly all week, and each time the instructions of his master came to mind, he grew uneasy. How did the Lord Baron envisage the transplanting of such trees?

He thus thought to contact him and found him in the library, engrossed in some type of reference books. As he gently broke it to him that centuries-old oaks can no longer be transplanted—that he had no idea how it was supposed to be done—the Lord Baron smiled patronizingly and asked that he retrieve the large green book out of the bookcase.

"This is a gardening book, dear sir," explained the Lord Baron in a kindly manner, "open it to where the marker is, and you will see that it can be done; it is illustrated with pictures. Inform yourself!"

And the caretaker read: "How to transplant a fuchsia shrub. Take the fuchsia out of the flowerpot and place it, along with all the roots, into the new one. Caution must be exercised when repotting to ensure that the roots are not damaged."

"Thus you see how simply it is done, my dear sir. You shall have the oaks dug up and place them in the location that I will specify. We shall have great holes excavated and place the oaks into them—that can be done with ease. I have grand schemes for how I shall reconfigure my estate. No doubt you must review my plans and implement them tirelessly, otherwise the work shall lag. Admittedly, this will appear onerous at first glance—scarcely feasible even—just like the business with these oaks, but we do have sufficient technical literature on hand. Begin with the oldest oak tree in front of the manor. Be cautious with the roots: every root must be gently unearthed from the soil. One must treat the oaks precisely as one would a fuchsia, oak and fuchsia—both are plants!"

The Lord Baron took pleasure in his lecture, and the caretaker did not contradict him.

"I wish to have all the oaks at the edge of the lake behind the manor, or—better yet—we shall dry out the lake and rear oaks instead of fish. We shall install benches all around the lake, and there I shall have a rest following my arduous labors. Now another thing occurs to me: if the oaks are just about to blossom, we may not transplant them—that is to say, it is indicated in the book that one must not repot a fuchsia while it is in bloom. But I suppose my apprehensions are needless now in autumn; only one thing causes me quite a headache: a fuchsia is meant to be repotted in a warm space, and yet one cannot do this with oaks, even though they are also sensitive to the cold. But a perfect solution has occurred to me. During the transplanting, we shall heat the soil surrounding the oaks and erect, to this end—following the draining dry of the lake—a small brick oven, by which the topsoil can be warmed before being shoveled into the pits, over the roots. The transplanting should occur during the daytime. Not even the fuchsia should be repotted at night, so that the green of the leaves not be adversely affected thereby. I also reckon that, in the course of transplanting, rain could cause harm to the oaks, and therefore, in the event of rain, the workers must climb the trees with umbrellas and sit aloft in the treetops with umbrellas spread, until it has ceased to rain and the work is complete. And I would like to discuss still one other matter with you. There, where the oaks have stood, we shall plant date palms. What a delight it will be when we reap the first harvest! From an economic standpoint, it would actually be more advantageous to plant only dates. I have given this matter much thought and discovered how one might really boost the local economy. Why does no one plant dates in this region? Out of a lack of industriousness! The dates growing on our estate will be shipped all over the world! After all, the soil is very good here. Yesterday I was out in the fields and was pleasantly surprised. I thought to myself, 'what lovely beets those are,' and the foreman said to me 'with your permission, Lord Baron, those are no beets—those are potatoes.' From this, I draw the lesson of how fine the land is here, if one mistakes potatoes for beets. However, the potato stalks were very dry and cracked. Next year, therefore, every potato plant must be fastened to a long stake, just as one does with hops or grapevines. This will be beneficial because the potato will then grow as a bush and need not be dug up. First, this makes for faster harvesting, and the potatoes remain clean as well. Everyone will be convinced of the expediency of such a way of doing business. We must also be economical with arable fields. Why the devil is wheat sown on one plot, rye on another, oats on a third, and barley on a fourth? You shall abandon this practice, caretaker, and henceforth mix all types of grain seeds and then crop them so that all types flourish next to one another, on a single plot. Space will be saved thereby, and one need not thresh wheat on one day, rye on the second, oats on the third, and barley on the fourth. Time will also be spared thereby, and in wintertime, when people have nothing more to do in the fields, they can sort through the harvested grains and toss them into four separate piles. Later, we shall want to take various precautionary measures, above all against hailstorms; we shall grow the grain beneath great sheds or canopies; we will also want to sow cocoa and coffee on the southern slopes, and millet and pearl barley as well. The farm is very neglected, but I hope that with our collective fortitude, we can manage before long to bring it to complete fruition. We must also proceed more practicably in connection with the poultry. We must breed the chickens to be larger, namely crossbreed geese and chickens and pay heed so that the roosters do not eat the chicks once the hens have given birth to them, as occasionally happens with pigs. Pigs wallow in the mud, become unsightly, and the flavor quality of the meat is degraded. For this reason, you must coat the pigs with enamel and allow them to dry for a few days near an oven. Pigs, which only roll in filth because their light color displeases them, cease to wallow and grow spirited again as soon as they are lacquered in black. For the cows, you must construct steam baths, so that they yield more milk; if the cows are healthier, the milk will also be more flavorful. So my dear master caretaker, farewell, think about what I have discussed, and commence with the work conscientiously."

Shortly thereafter, the good caretaker walked into the lake!

1912

Saved

Why Pátal was condemned to death by hanging is entirely irrelevant. Whatever the nature of his crime, he could not suppress a smile, when, on the eve of the morning he was to be executed, in accordance with the law, the jailer brought into his cell a bottle of wine and a proper piece of roast veal.

"That belongs to me?"

"Yes indeed," replied the jailer sympathetically, "so that you might enjoy a final meal. There is also cucumber salad besides. I couldn't carry it all at once. I'll be right back and bring rolls as well. I shall only be a moment."

Jaroslav Hašek

Pátal made himself comfortable at the table, smiling with delight as he bit into the roast veal. It was plain to see that he was a cynic but otherwise an entirely sensible man, who still wished to enjoy what the world had to offer during the final few hours of life granted him by the courts.

Only a single thought tainted the meal for him somewhat: namely, the thought all those people who had, that morning, delivered to him the ruling that his appeal for clemency had been denied and that the fulfillment of the sentence would follow in twenty-four hours, allowing the condemned to settle his legal affairs, in preparation for the carrying out of the punishment in accordance with the law—that all the people who were to hang and execute him and be in attendance at his death—all of them would live on peacefully with their families tomorrow, the next day, and thereafter, whereas he would cease to exist.

Thus did he philosophize over the roast veal, and as the rolls and cucumber salad were brought to him, he sighed and expressed his desire for a pipe and tobacco. And, so he could enjoy a pleasant smoke, a pipe and Three King's Tobacco—a mélange of normal tobacco and mild leaf—were purchased for him. The warden even gave him a light, thus reminding him of God's endless mercy. Even if all was lost here on earth, it was certainly not yet so in heaven.

Saved

The condemned Pátal asked for a portion of ham and a liter of wine.

"You shall receive what you desire," said the warden. "One must fulfill every wish of a man in your situation."

"Bring me two liverwurst as well, and a portion of aspic. I would also like a liter of dark beer."

"You shall receive it all, it will be fetched promptly," the warden responded politely. "Why should you be denied the pleasure? Life is too brief not to be enjoyed at every opportunity."

Once he had brought the desired items, they continued to philosophize together, and Pátal declared that he was fully satisfied.

"Gosh!" he exclaimed, once he had devoured it all, "now I have a hankering for roast Debrecziner,[1] gorgonzola cheese, sardines in oil, and other good things."

"You shall receive all that you desire. Truth be told, I'm glad you're enjoying it. I hope you won't hang yourself before the morning. You certainly wouldn't do that to me. After all, I see that you're an honest fellow. What good would it do you, Mr. Pátal, were you to hang yourself before it happens in accordance with the law? I tell you as a candid man, on my word, that you cannot accomplish it as effectively—never, no comparison! Would you like another glass of beer or two? It is excellent

---

1. A type of seasoned pork sausage popular throughout Central Europe, named after the Hungarian city of Debrecen.

today. It tastes exquisite paired with gorgonzola. I shall bring you two more glasses, and with the sardines and roast Debrecziner, you shall drink wine, dear friend; that pairing is more suitable!"

A short time later, the aroma of all those things filled the cell, and in the midst of such abundance, Pátal sat and feasted voraciously, first on the cheese, then on the sardines, and drank, alternately, beer or wine—whichever found its way into his hand.

He became lost in happy memories of similar luxuries in freedom, of having spent an evening on the veranda of a beer garden, where the branches and leaves shimmered in the sunlight before the window, and across from him had sat the publican of this paradise—a man similar in girth to the warden—chatting constantly and calling for food and drink, just like this warden.

"Tell me a story," Pátal entreated him, and the warden eagerly shared some new anecdote of swinish content, as he himself admitted.

Then Pátal expressed his desire for fruit and tarts or confections and a cup of black coffee.

His wish was fulfilled.

Once he had conquered this, the prison chaplain turned up to console Pátal.

He was a cheerful companion, not condescending but pleasant, like all the people who now cared for him, who had condemned him to death, and who would, tomorrow, hang him; all of them had cheerful faces and were certainly very genial in their social intercourse.

"God comfort you, my son," said the prison chaplain, patting him on the shoulder. "Tomorrow morning, it will all be over, have no doubt. Confess, and look about cheerfully at the world with trust in God, because God is pleased with every sinner who repents. There are men who do not confess their sins, then run about the whole night and moan; I know it isn't pleasant when one is overwhelmed, but he who has confessed sleeps the sleep of the just on the last night—he is comforted! I say to you once more, my son, that you too will feel comforted if you unburden your soul from sin."

At that moment, Pátal went pale, his stomach rebelled, he felt nauseous, and he vomited. Yet that was not the end of it; he developed stomach cramps, and a cold sweat formed on his brow.

The prison chaplain grew frightened. More cramps set in. Pátal convulsed with pain in the corner of his cell.

The warden carried him to the prison hospital ward. The court physicians shook their heads. In the evening, he was stricken with fever, and at midnight the doctors declared his condition critical and stated unanimously that this was a case of poisoning.

Condemned persons who are critically ill are not to be hanged; therefore, the gallows were not erected that night.

Instead, Pátal's stomach was flushed out, and an analysis of the leftovers revealed rancidity in the liverwurst, found when pan after pan of undigested remnants were pumped from Pátal's stomach.

It was hypothesized that the liverwurst had undergone chemical degradation in the heat, and that the resultant rancidity was the source of the grave illness.

An investigation was promptly conducted at the butcher shop that had delivered the liverwurst, and it was found that the good butcher had flouted health regulations, having not placed the liverwurst on ice. The matter was handed over to a public prosecutor, and he initiated the proper measures against the butcher, for the endangerment of public health.

Among the court physicians who treated Pátal was a young, ambitious doctor, who studied the illness assiduously and was keenly devoted to keeping Pátal alive, because the case was especially challenging and interesting.

He cared for Pátal painstakingly, day and night, until, after fourteen days, he could pat him on the shoulder and inform him "*You are saved.*"

On the following day, Pátal was hanged in accordance with the law, as his physical constitution was by then capable of enduring the noose.

However, the butcher, who had lengthened Pátal's life by fourteen days with his liverwurst, was sentenced to

Saved

three weeks' hard time for endangering public safety.

The doctor who had saved Pátal's life received a commendation from the court.

1910

Justice Prevails

Fantastical things occur in this world; and yet truth and justice ultimately prevail—of this Mr. Vačkář had long been convinced. To say that justice carries the day only in particular cases was hardly adequate in his view.

Anyone might reasonably suspect that this notion of justice refers to the appropriate disposition of the police, of the entire constabulary, and—continuing on, step by step—of the court, the prison, the gallows, and so forth.

When it comes to this so-called justice, one gets the distinct impression that it concludes, in the best-case scenario, with a dry newspaper article, and that settles the matter.

Mr. Vačkář happily contemplates such cases and recounts, with a smiling countenance, one that he himself experienced.

Years ago, he owned a haberdashery that was situated in a remote alleyway, into which police patrols strayed only on the rarest of occasions. At that time, the number of nightly store break-ins had increased, and not a single day passed during which at least one business wasn't robbed by some insolent means. As the burglaries piled up, to such a degree that police stations would be forced, for this reason, to deploy special auxiliary forces, the police headquarters came to the realization that police patrols must devote particular attention at night to thieves. This simple and useful directive was crowned with success!

One day, Mr. Vačkář worked until midnight, taking inventory, and then stepped out of his business with a ball of fabric, intending to have it shipped early the following morning.

Two policemen, who had already observed him before he turned out the light, adhering to their official instructions, confronted him immediately after he had carefully locked up his store. And even as he declared that he was the owner of the business, the policemen laughed at this threadbare alibi and escorted him to the nearest police station. The commissioner likewise laughed at the clumsy excuse and was of the opinion that Mr. Vačkář simply was not a skilled burglar. Another police official joined in, asking with veiled sarcasm: "You were taking inventory, no? That's typically the case in a burglary!"

"But I really was taking inventory...", said a fearful Mr. Vačkář, attempting to defend himself.

"And thus you shall do time," the official assured him.

And because the order had been given that all arrested burglars should be measured, photographed, and finger-printed at the station, they placed Mr. Vačkář in handcuffs, linking his left hand to the right hand of another rascal (as they now called him), and led them both in this fashion to police headquarters.

"Just don't tell the truth," advised the criminal.

"Hadn't crossed my mind," replied a sheepish Mr. Vačkář, which incriminated him greatly thereafter.

He cried while having his picture taken, resulting in the need for multiple photographs.

Measurement of his skull circumference proved a demonstrative criminal predisposition, which was established by a chart of Lombrosian theory.[1] According to another chart, the curvature of the forehead and the form of the nose attested to extraordinary degeneracy,

---

1. Cesare Lombroso (1835–1909) was an influential Italian criminologist and physician. Using theories of Social Darwinism, he posited that criminal behavior was an inherited trait, one that could be physically identified using pseudoscientific techniques such as phrenology.

dissolution, and sexual perversity. The thumbprint matched that of a thief and murderer from Mannheim by the name of König (this name was underlined in black, reflecting the fact that the man had already died by execution some five years prior). The fingerprints matched those of the renowned international fraudster Rubinstein, of the pickpocket Futerka, of the burglar Zálinsky, of the swindler Semerádova, and of the child murderer Zinková.

As these results were made known, Mr. Vačkář broke into a fit of tears once more, for he had heard it said many times that no two thumbprints are ever alike, and he asserted that he was neither the Semerádova woman nor the one named Zinková.

"Of that, one cannot yet be so certain," he was told sternly, and now he broke into a fit of twitching, reminiscent of persons afflicted with rheumatic fever. On the following morning, he was transferred to the prison hospital ward, as he appeared to have developed meningitis—the old malingerer. In the hospital ward, he hovered between life and death for two days, during which Mr. Vačkář's housekeeper reported the mysterious disappearance of her employer to the police. There, they laid before her one of the photographs in which Mr. Vačkář appeared so pitiable.

"That is not him," the housekeeper stated in the course of the proceedings, confidently providing her signature on a declaration. She had no desire whatsoever to visit the rascal in the jail.

Meanwhile, in the hospital ward, Mr. Vačkář had recovered enough that the magistrate could be dispatched to interrogate him.

"Where have you hidden the corpse of Mr. Vačkář, whom you murdered?"

"I recall nothing of the sort, your honor," replied a stunned Mr. Vačkář.

"What's your name?" the magistrate questioned further.

"I don't know any more, I have been told that I am not Vačkář."

"*And that you are not*," retorted the magistrate. "Now, how much money did you find in the register?"

"About thirty gulden," replied the convalescent patient.

The magistrate left in order to confirm this. The description corresponded to the amount that had been found on the accused at the time of his arrest. Meanwhile, the public followed, with bated breath, daily reports about the mysterious murder of a man whose existence was unknown to them prior to that fateful day, and whose name now appeared in all the newspapers. It was simply astonishing that, in his lucid moments, the accused related to the magistrate the life of the vanished merchant, with such precision as to prove beyond any doubt that he must have known the victim very well.

Finally, he was in a sufficiently healthy condition that he could be brought before his housekeeper, who attested to having seen the man somewhere before—perhaps even outside the business of the murder victim. There were several more witnesses besides, who declared concordantly that this haggard, hoary man resembled someone who had frequently stood in front of the business of the vanished Mr. Vačkář.

At times, so the magistrate observed, the accused reverted to his old form of trickery, which was perhaps singular in the history of crime: the assertion that he himself was the missing and murdered person. To confuse the suspect, the magistrate had him write "I am Josef Vačkář, who resides in the New Alley." The handwriting was compared with that of the missing merchant, and the court counselors declared unanimously that the writing samples resembled one another in no respect whatsoever, and the slanting quality of the one sample was an unmistakable indication of alcoholism.

More and more, the accused gave the impression of an emotionally stunted person, and the magistrate observed with visible pleasure that Mr. Vačkář was now gradually admitting to his crimes, so much so that the former could one day enter into the record, to his great satisfaction, that, to the question of "Who owned the clothing you were wearing on the day of your arrest?" Mr. Vačkář responded, "Mr. Josef Vačkář."

That he had spoken the truth in this case was confirmed by the housekeeper as well as other witnesses, who had seen Mr. Vačkář going to and from his business in such attire.

One day, the suspect confessed that Mr. Vačkář had a brother, who was employed in the forestry administration in the Nitra region of Hungary.

"Surely you are aware," said the magistrate, "that we will have him summoned by telegraph and bring him to confront you."

"Do with me what you wish," replied the suspect despondently, "we have not seen one another for twenty years."

Three days later, the brother of the vanished person stood before him, eye to eye. For five minutes he studied his face intently, before hugging the accused and exclaiming, "Josef, what a state I've found you in!" The accused smiled, shrugged, and said coolly: "I am not your brother, I am no longer Josef Vačkář!"

Yet his brother swore that the man *was* Josef Vačkář, and the court doctors determined that Mr. Josef Vačkář must no longer be entirely sane, and that it was indeed Josef Vačkář who had stepped out of his business that evening and who, for the last three months, had found himself under interrogation by the criminal court. His housekeeper and the other witnesses realized their small errors, which had occurred in the interest of justice, and, one after the other, confirmed under oath that the suspect was in fact the missing merchant.

The charge of murder, which he was supposed to have perpetrated against himself, was dropped, thus leaving only the investigation into the theft of the fabric ball that was found on his person. This investigation was suspended, however, due to a lack of evidence.

Another two years passed before the asylum doctors managed to cure him of the obsessive conviction that he was not Josef Vačkář, whose burgled corpse he had hidden.

And once they declared him recovered and released him after those two years, Mr. Vačkář grasped that justice really does prevail at the end of the day, in spite of many obstacles, and he proclaims this truth with great aplomb everywhere and to anyone who is willing to listen.

1911

The Apprentices of the Kobkán Shipping Company

The proprietor of the well-known Kobkán Shipping Company had Pecháček, an apprentice in the correspondence division, summoned to his office, and spoke with him at length.

As Pecháček returned to his desk, he was pale; his entire body trembled, and his hair stood on end.

"Notice of termination?" asked the accounting clerk.

In place of an answer, the apprentice Pecháček took his hat and winter jacket and left the office without a word. The accounting clerk went immediately to the director's office; as he returned, he shook his head and said: "I really don't understand it. The boss gave him the entire afternoon off, to spend at a wine tavern."

Five apprentices looked with envy at Pecháček's empty chair and then immersed themselves once more in their calculations.

A strange mood spread throughout the office of the Kobkán Shipping Company; something mysterious, enigmatic, and incomprehensible had happened.

At the same time, what transpired was quite ordinary, if also a bit unusual. The director had had a friendly conversation with Pecháček. He said: "Mr. Pecháček, you are a young, gifted person. The manager and the accounting clerk praise you highly. You are diligent, humble, versatile, judicious, good-natured, and industrious. You neither drink, nor smoke, nor play cards, nor behave inappropriately towards women. You are not in debt, you take no advances on your wages, you can numerate and calculate well, you have fine penmanship, you waste no paper, you arrive at the office punctually, and you are the last to go home. You have a mind for business, you write quickly and flexibly in shorthand, you type without error on every typewriter, regardless of the apparatus. You know several languages, and you dress modestly but properly. Your shoes are always carefully polished and the collars of your shirts are always clean…"

In bliss, the exemplary apprentice grew teary-eyed, and he looked, transfixed, at his boss, who looked at his apprentice with an endearing, kind-hearted gaze and said with a soft voice: "My name day[1] is fourteen days away. It would make me so happy on that occasion to see well-wishes in the newspapers from my staff, friends, and acquaintances. It goes without saying that I, myself, will cover the associated expenses. However, I would like the well-wishes for the occasion not to be run-of-the-mill. I desire something unique—let us say something written in the style of a shipping agent. Something that has not been done before. Something lovely, so that years later the reader will still recall the well-wishes for my name day. Something that everyone will find moving. And for this reason, I thought of you. It goes without saying that you should not mention anything about this to anyone. Let me shake your hand."

The apprentice extended his trembling hand to the director, who shook it and continued: "So you shall do it. Today is a lovely sunny day that will inspire you. Therefore, I am giving you the entire afternoon off. Go to a wine tavern and drink a half liter of muscat or vermouth, so you can versify more successfully. I know you will not drink to excess. Then

---

1. In Czech culture, each day of the year corresponds to a particular first name or names. On a name day, small gifts are given and celebrations held for the person of honor. The tradition originated from liturgical calendars and the feast days of saints. Once popular throughout Catholic and Orthodox countries, and often more important than birthday celebrations, name day customs are still celebrated in modern Czechia.

go to Stromovka Park[2], sit on a bench there, and compose the well-wishes for my name day. Here's fifty crowns."

And so it happened that Pecháček, white as chalk, returned to his desk. He complied with the first and the second part of his instructions precisely.

Like a machine, he went to the wine tavern and drank a quarter liter of muscat and the same of vermouth—not excessively—and went to the park. There he sat down on a bench and began to write.

To his horror, he found that he did not feel inspired, and every capacity that his director attributed to him as a gifted apprentice was simply inaccessible—that neither a lovely sunny day nor muscat and vermouth could help.

"Christ above," he sighed, "what rubbish I've written—there's nothing original about it whatsoever. Why, is it not nonsense to write: 'Hear our most inner wishes, that your life's fullness be as rich as the heavens are full of stars. Of your work, daily successes under this firmament. Happiness and long life, one success succeeding the next. Many years of joy and happiness ahead, that every wish be fulfilled—so wish all of your acquaintances, friends, and staff.'"

---

2. Established in the 13th century as royal a game preserve, Stromovka is a large park in the Bubeneč district of Prague, north of the city center. It lies on the floodplain of the Vltava River and is protected as a national monument.

The Apprentices

Pecháček tore the composed well-wishes out of his notebook, ripped them up, and tossed them in a waste-basket, then contemplated further and wrote.

Countless name day well-wishes filled the pages of the notebook:

"This year, too, our wishes are ones of good fortune for you, we wish you wholeheartedly an entire year of the very finest once again. Daily naught but pleasures and the best, health and good things aplenty. Moving trucks at half price, also the greatest comforts with the noble wife and the family—so wish your acquaintances, friends, and staff."

"May the cornucopia bring you only exuberant friends and a long life. Success and happiness, numerous transactions with the noble wife, and best wishes experienced in delight. Your acquaintances, friends, and staff wish you that wholeheartedly."

"May business blossom in pure delights and without distress to you. May your life flow as blissfully as a calm brook. May the Lord bless you with a long life. Success in every endeavor. That there be no illness. That the raising of shipping tariffs not be on the horizon—so desire all the acquaintances, friends, and staff, on all accounts."

Further into the notebook appeared suggestions for rhymes: place–grace, good–could, sing–bring, name–fame, venerate–generate.

The unfortunate apprentice crossed everything out, tore up his notes, tossed them, and went to the next park, where he held his head in his hands.

"I'm daft, an idiot, nothing but a halfwit; my brain is melting. Something original in the style of a shipping agent. My dim-witted skull! An idiot I am, I've lost my mind! Intelligent? An ox! Naught but straw for brains!"

He attempted to find inspiration in a tavern with the aid of a bottle of wine. In place of the anticipated eureka moment arose such a fit of stupidity that he wrote:

"On this day so precious, we wish from the heart a life of further fortune, and that you may be constantly joyous at all times. May only well-being blossom and success stream upon all endeavors, long years of health and an abundance of flowers be seen from your windows. So wish wholeheartedly your acquaintances, friends, and staff."

"Finished," he said, laughing dully at his lines, "I'm a mongrel, a mundane dullard, and degenerate."

In the early morning, his hat was found on the causeway of the sluice at Klecany. In the hat lay a piece of paper with his address and the words: "I can't..." and nothing more.

At the office, the five apprentices discussed the mysterious suicide of their colleague, Pecháček. They spoke softly, with a fitting degree of sorrow, because they missed him—good, dependable Pecháček.

The office attendant appeared and said: "Apprentice Klofanda to the director's office!"

The Apprentices

"I'm coming!"

The director said: "Mr. Klofanda, you are a young, gifted person. The manager and the accounting clerk praise you highly. You are diligent, versatile, judicious, humble, honest, and industrious."

And so on, to the point of "Here's fifty crowns."

As Klofanda returned to his desk, he was pale; his entire body trembled, his hair stood on end, he said nothing, and he left the office, taking hat and coat.

The atmosphere of the enigmatic, the mysterious, and the unknown grew thicker still.

The remaining four apprentices shook their heads.

Klofanda possessed less of the writer's gift than the dearly departed Pecháček, but he was a pure, tender, and responsible soul. Meditate as he might, nothing occurred to him. Before he hanged himself that night in the Hodkovičky forest, he had managed to muster nothing more than: "It is our most heartfelt wish to convey to you our most sincere well-wishes; all of your acquaintances, friends, and staff wish this."

"I alone am responsible for my death," he wrote on a piece of paper that he tucked into his winter jacket.

The four apprentices in the office had not yet fully discussed the curious death of their second colleague, when the office attendant appeared once again: "Apprentice Vencl to the director!"

"I'm coming!"

And then said the director: "Mr. Vencl, you are diligent, versatile, judicious, humble, good-natured, and industrious."

And so on, to the point of "Here's fifty crowns."

The atmosphere of the enigmatic, the mysterious, and the unknown thickened yet again. A faint smell of death wafted through the office.

Apprentice Vencl came up with absolutely nothing. He died at the Prague stone quarries, where he slit his wrists, leaving behind not a single line of text.

"Apprentice Košťák to the director!" …

"I'm coming!"

Košťák resisted death for a time. For two full days he hid in the gardens of Petřín Hill, and only on the third day did he jump from the scenic overlook there. At that point, he was already thoroughly deranged and was under the impression that his director was no shipping agent but rather a merchant dealing in live birds, and that he needed to compose well-wishes for a silver wedding anniversary.

That explained also why, on one page of his notebook, the following note was found: "That happy times may bloom, that the silver wedding anniversary should recur every year, that business may prosper, and that a thousand doves, rabbits, and fish are sold profitably. So wishes your Jan Košťák."

At the office of Mr. Kobkán only two apprentices remained.

"Apprentice Havlík to the director!" …

"I'm coming!"

Once he had written his original well-wish in the form of a business telegram— "Kobkán, shipping agent…birthday…heartfelt congratulations…acquaintances…friends…the staff"—he impaled himself with a pocket knife in the restroom of the Municipal House.[3]

"Apprentice Pilař to the director!"

The last of the apprentices remaining at the Kóbkan shipping firm went pale. He had an uncertain premonition that behind the door of the director's office lay the source of that enormous tragedy that had befallen the apprentices of this shipping firm, a tragedy that was simply incomprehensible, and he sensed that the enigmatic, the mysterious, and the unknown now approached him as well.

"Apprentice Pilař to the director immediately!" repeated the office attendant.

The final apprentice stood up and cried out in despair: "I'm not going!"

---

3. A large civic building in central Prague, built in the Art Nouveau style and opened in 1912. It houses a café, a ballroom, a concert hall, and offices for civil servants.

There were four pale faces in the office: that of the apprentice, the manager, the accounting clerk, and the office attendant.

"Mr. Pilař," the accounting clerk said questioningly, "consider what you are saying. It is unheard of in Bohemia that an apprentice will not go when the director calls him."

"I won't go," repeated the last apprentice despairingly, "I'm not going anywhere."

The director himself appeared in the doorway. "Mr. Pilař, come into the office. I have had you called twice already."

"I won't go!" cried the last apprentice, "when I say to you that I won't go, I won't go."

He began to gesticulate wildly with his hands and cried, "Everyone is gone, the dearly departed Pecháček, the dearly departed Klofanda, the dearly departed Vencl, the dearly departed Košťák, the dearly departed Havlík. Only I go not, I'm not going anywhere."

He took hold of a heavy ledger book and slammed it on the table.

"I shall remain seated, I will not go anywhere, I will smash everything, I will batter everyone to death. I am Captain Mora, world sensation and unsurpassed in the aviation scene.[4] I fear you not!"

---

4. A now-obscure reference to a character in the popular novel *Galeon Kapitana Mory*, written by the Polish author Jerzy Bohdan Rychliński.

The Apprentices

The medical personnel had no complaints about the last apprentice of the Kobkán firm. On his straitjacket were five buttons, and he pointed to the buttons, counted, and said: "The first is Klofanda, the second is Vencl, the third Košt'ák, the fourth Havlík, the fifth Pecháček. No, that's not right. The first is Pecháček, the second is Klofanda, the third is Vencl, the fourth Košt'ák, the fifth Havlík. Everyone went, but I go not, I'm not going anywhere!"

The doctors slowly lost hope that he could be rehabilitated. The name day of Mr. Kobkán passed without original well-wishes in the newspaper. In the office sit six fresh apprentices. The police have only until the proprietor's next name day to explain the mysterious die-off of apprentices at the Kobkán Shipping Company.

1921

The Footrace

While roaming through Hungary prior to the Great War, I passed through Nagykanizsa, where I found a brewery with a Czech brewmaster, 120 meters of old fortress walls, and the grave of some vizier or other from the time when Nagykanizsa was the residence of the Turkish pasha, surrounded by a sea of infidel mercenaries led by Prince Eugene. The Little Abbé, as that butcher was known, launched such a valiant mortar barrage on the town that a cannonball ripped the vizier's head off in the marketplace. The turban that he bore upon his head is now found in the museum of Nagykanizsa, but it strikes me as quite suspect. I fear it is the same deception as the one that we in Bohemia peddle with the tongue of Saint John of Nepomuk.[1] It appears very fresh. In the city museum are also displayed the bones of the camel on which the vizier sat when that misfortune befell him. Here, the deception is as clear as day. Only an atrophied sheep could have such thin and tiny bones.

Apart from this, there is nothing of note in Nagykanizsa. Dust lies on the streets, and on the city outskirts, to which gardens extend, there buzz aggressive swarms of mosquitoes. One week before I arrived, embezzlement was discovered for roughly the tenth time at city hall, and this ended court sessions for the year, which featured approximately eight local robbery-homicides and 32 major cases of fraud. The cultural *niveau* had risen to quite a height.

There were also mosquitoes in the city park, and the local officials permitted gypsies to play "Úram, úram, bíró, úram…" (Lord, lord, lord, judge…) in the park restaurant without pause. An imbecilic song, and nauseating.

---

1. A reference to the medieval saint of Bohemia, who was drowned at the behest of King Wenceslas IV, allegedly for refusing to divulge what the queen said at confession. Several hundred years later, when his body was disinterred, his tongue was said to have been preserved undecayed. This pseudo-relic, no longer generally believed, is nevertheless still housed in a sumptuous reliquary at St. Vitus Cathedral in Prague.

The Footrace

One does not remain in such a city for long. I managed to find a hotel where the bugs of Nagykanizsa and its environs appeared to be holding congress. The room I received distinguished itself by an utter lack of elegance. It contained a washing trough, a trash receptacle, and—in place of a washbasin—a jug.

This so annoyed me that I went again to the city park, where I got to know a young woman from a respectable family of civil servants. I introduced myself as a millionaire who traversed Europe by foot out of sheer boredom. My name would surely be familiar to her: *Gordon Bennett.*[2]

She was so very pleased that I spoke a little Hungarian. I permitted myself to be invited to dinner with the family and sent some dame from her household to fetch my knapsack full of dirty laundry from the hotel.

The young lady's father was a good-natured, proper gentleman and the wife-mother a credulous creature. In Vasz, where there are vineyards, they had an uncle—one who owned wine cellars—and therefore they had good wine aplenty at their disposal in this home.

As I grew drunk, I promised to take Etelka as my wife—just as soon as I finished traversing the globe by foot.

---

2. "Gordon Bennett" was a period expression, meaning doubt or incredulity, that referenced the American sportsman and publisher James Gordon Bennett Jr.

Later, once I was in the spirit, I pledged before the portraits of her grandfather and grandmother, which hung in the dining room, that no Hungarian king possessed so lovely a villa as I would build for my Etelka on Lake Balaton.

Then her father *had* to promise me he would take a leave of absence from his job tomorrow morning and accompany me on foot through Hungary to Turkey, ensuring that I did not go astray. I was fed lavishly and carried to bed. I awoke just before noon and perceived an extraordinary bustle in the adjacent room. There was much rummaging about; I heard the opening and closing of drawers.

I was still lounging in bed when, after a brief knock, the father of Miss Etelka walked in. "Mr. Gordon Bennett," he told me, "everything is already prepared, finalized, and in order. The health insurance doctor examined me for some time, but finally he prescribed me two-month's holiday for a trip to the south. I already have the papers in order. The women have prepared my linens as well as the touring provisions. They are baking us chickens for the trip, and tomorrow morning we shall set off through Hungary towards Turkey. What destination do you think we shall continue onward to?"

Gradually, I came to my senses.

"We shall have ourselves ferried across the Bosporus towards Asia Minor," I replied, "we shall hike across it in its entirety and go from Mesopotamia to Persia. We will scale the Himalayan mountains, bringing us to India. And then, across China, Korea, Kamchatka, through the Bering Strait, to North America, and from there towards South America and Patagonia. From Patagonia we shall embark for Australia. Clear across Australia and then by ship to South Africa. We will land at the Cape of Good Hope and then go northward, ever northward through all of Africa to Morocco. From Morocco to Gibraltar and ever farther northward over Spain to France. Then we shall veer eastward across Switzerland, Tyrol, Styria, bringing us once more to Nagykanizsa. And, if it suits you, we can rest for two or three days and then tramp to Iceland, Greenland, the North Pole and over Siberia back home. Do you wish to visit Madagascar?"

He scratched himself behind the ear, asking with some uncertainty "Is that really the largest lake in Australia?"

I nodded my head: "The largest and the deepest, but it dries out regularly every five thousand years."

That day, I spent a few untroubled hours with Etelka in the garden. Between kisses, I contemplated how I could disappear from this place.

If worse comes to worst, I'll outrun Mr. Cendes when we depart tomorrow, on the outskirts of the city. I'll ditch my knapsack and run away, with a strenuous burst of speed, in the direction of Balaton.

In Etelka's mind reigned a confused tangle of geographic notions. In Mr. Cendes' case, I am convinced that he at least knew what Africa is. If it perhaps escaped his memory that Africa was a continent, he at least held it to be a country of sorts.

However, as I expanded upon my travel itinerary before the gentle creature, I grew convinced that India, Korea, Australia, and also Kamchatka had not disturbed the pollen of her innocence. In backwardness, she was behind even the ancient Herodotus, who, no doubt, surmised that there existed still other lands besides Greece.

The time between lunch and dinner elapsed quickly amid bold promises. I promised her the prepared trunk of an Indian elephant, the pelts of all carnivores, Richard Andree's *World Atlas*, the skulls of the inhabitants of Polynesia, Indian scalps, diamonds from the Cape Province and rubies from Mount Kilimanjaro, golden necklaces from Peru and Chile, the roof from the palace of the Tibetan Dalai Lama, the glass eye of the Japanese emperor, living Chinese and Eskimo couples, an entire tribe from Zambezi, and so on.

The poor creature was happy and asked me the most miscellaneous questions. The most incredible of these was whether the waterlines were functioning properly in New Zealand (it bears mentioning that the week before there had been complications with the municipal pipelines in Nagykanizsa). With naive charm, she proposed: "Let's wager that I can guess correctly where the Caspian Sea flows." The particulars have since vanished from my mind, but I can vouch that if a cold-blooded geography professor had been in my place, he would have strangled her.

The supper proceeded ceremoniously. With this meal, Mr. Cendes took leave of his family. I can assure you that I spoke little of my riches. I merely insinuated. "Had I one hundred times as much wealth, I could not, after all, buy myself true happiness or another cup of chocolate."

My torn shoes provoked admiration: "The hippopotamus, from which my shoes are made," I said, "I slew on the Nile, and they are the best proof that even hippopotamus hide can grow worn out. The assertions of experts regarding the durability of hippopotamus hide are simply preposterous!"

"It is interesting," I continued, pointing to the patches on the elbows of my jacket, "that the aristocratic women of the greatest tourist clubs in all of England cannot repair jackets, even though I hiked ten times around England in its entirety."

Would you please throw me out already? I thought to myself, as I observed with disquietude how the whole family hung on my every word, taking everything at face value. *Or if you would at least sic the police on me…*

Instead, they posed the most miscellaneous questions: "Are your parents still alive?"

"Father," I replied, "read Jules Vernes' novel, *From the Earth to the Moon*, and wanted to put its plot into practice. He had a mortar manufactured and launched himself at the moon in a rocket. Eight years have passed since then, and he has yet to return. We have received no word from him. Mother rode in her yacht, *Torpedo*, to the South Sea in search of him and now floats through the ocean upon an ice floe."

Now I'm cooked, I thought with confidence, but instead Etelka asked, "Have you no sister?"

"My sister married the President of the United States," I answered, "but she is unhappy with him because she has fallen in love with the famous singer, Caruso, for whom she purchased a ranch in Sumatra for the rearing of tigers and jaguars."

Now they must surely phone the police, I thought.

"Everyone has their troubles," said Mrs. Cendes, gazing at me with a heartfelt, motherly look. "Such things happen in all families. Have you a brother?"

"My brother is an eccentric. He gave away his entire, vast fortune and is now a clerk at the Slavia Bank in Prague."

Now they'll throw me out, I said to myself assuredly, but instead Mr. Cendes brought to utterance "Where will you and Etelka go honeymooning when we return?"

"To Zanzibar and Arabia," I answered. "It is too warm in Italy. Besides, the Arabs are a hospitable people."

The Footrace

I imbibed so much that I could have sustained forests in the Sahara Desert thereby, and hoped I would succeed in developing a case of delirium tremens, so I would be taken to the hospital. Instead, I fell asleep on my stool. I was gently put to bed.

*

Mr. Cendes woke me first thing in the morning. He was already completely prepared to set out, and his tubby figure gave his tourist getup a comical effect. After breakfast, at which Mrs. Cendes and Etelka did not merely cry but rather bawled from deep within, we left the house and hit the road towards Balaton.

They accompanied us, amid ceaseless lamentation and howling, to the city's last garden.

"Look after Mr. Gordon Bennett," admonished Mrs. Cendes for a final time, and we were left alone. Before us stretched the plains to Lake Balaton; the white, dusty country road curved endlessly into the distance. The dust clung thickly to the mulberry bushes, the sun-wilted grass appeared sad and withered, and in my mind ripened a plan of escape.

"Are you a good runner?" I asked Mr. Cendes.

"An outstanding one, Mr. Gordon Bennett," he replied, "years ago, I started for the track and field club in Sopron."

I bit my lip. We came to a hill, the country road led upward. I began to run. I set out in a sprint.

Mr. Cendes ran up behind me and cried out "I understand you, Mr. Gordon Bennett—the first of us to Balaton: a forty-kilometer course!"

He closed in on me. I ran the first ten kilometers with a lead of no more and no less than ten meters. By the twelfth kilometer, before the village of Mezőlak, he caught up and ran right next to me. After fifteen kilometers, I overtook him by a solid fifty meters, which decreased to only five in the village of Botafal.

At the twenty-five-kilometer mark, we were running next to one another again, and, after thirty kilometers, at the village of Kapotfalva, I finally shook him. The lead amounted to a half kilometer. My energy was exhausted. I rested for a time, then ran onward. In the curve of the country road, there appeared Mr. Cendes and—roughly one hundred meters behind him—a man who was gradually gaining ground on him. Others could be seen running in the distance. I could not make sense of it, and I grew uneasy. I broke into a sprint.

A cyclist rode past me with a flag in his hand. He nodded amiably and asked "Which team are you on?"

I did not answer and continued running. After thirty-eight kilometers, I saw that the man who had been running behind Mr. Cendes had overtaken him and was now behind me.

I exerted what remained of my strength. Roaring like a locomotive, I ran past the first cottages of Balaton.

The Footrace

After forty kilometers, a huge crowd of people greeted me with joyous shouting. The band played "The Rákóczi March".[3]

I charged through the finish line that spanned across the lane, but I had not even the time to collapse onto the country road. I was snatched up and photographed, and fans of some sort hoisted me upon their shoulders and carried me into a hotel.

I was unable to say anything. I was pulled out and lugged into a pool. Then, the man who ran after me from kilometer thirty-eight was brought in. After five minutes Mr. Cendes appeared with his tongue hanging out and a happy smile. He came in third.

Through an unfortunate coincidence, the track and field club of Nagykanizsa had held a marathon race from Kanizsa to Balaton that very same day.

The matter was soon cleared up. They wanted to lynch us, and finally, on the order of a local official, gendarmes led us out of the city.

*

Only in Albania, where we were ambushed by bandits, did I rid myself of Mr. Cendes. I convinced

---

3 An unofficial anthem of Hungary during the Austro-Hungarian Empire, adapted by several 19th century composers, including Hector Berlioz, not to be confused with the "Radetzky March" by Johann Strauss Jr.

them that he was a famous millionaire and that they could expect to receive a vast ransom in exchange for him. They carried him off into the mountains, and as a sign of gratitude, they took only my knapsack full of dirty laundry.

Naturally, I know nothing of the fate of Mr. Cendes, because—sensitive as I am—I am ashamed to correspond with his unfortunate family in Nagykanizsa.

1921

Homage to an Abandoned Latrine

M an grows melancholy when forced to witness how all things go to rack and ruin—how the glory of yore dissipates.

The abandoned latrine on the former military training grounds at Dejvice is a depressing sight to behold. It lies at the foot of a mountain, where a pedestrian bridge spans the stream and a trail begins winding upward towards a shrine to St. Matthew. In bygone times, when the water level remained sufficiently high, the stream carried all the refuse that flowed out of the latrine in the direction of the zoological gardens. Oh, much water has passed under the bridge since the days when the drums sounded, the snorting and galloping of horses was heard, the gunfire of men's rifles roared, and the imperial flags fluttered on the fields of Dejvice.

The regiments disappeared long ago, the field has long since lost the blue hue given it by military uniforms, and all that remains here is an abandoned latrine and a few wooden planks meant to spare civilians the sight of what is contained within. The facility is comprised of two beams secured a short distance from one another, which did their duty well and truly; below is an engineered ditch, half filled with the black, dried-out leaves of the surrounding plum trees, whose upper branches bowed curiously inward. When the plum trees are in flower, the white blossoms fall into the abandoned latrine, just as the surrounding dandelions and daisies bloom, as if Mother Nature endeavors to bring cheer to the abandoned latrine, dispelling, with fresh blossoms, the gloom that emanates from this sad site.

On spring and autumn mornings and evenings, when fog rolls into the Vltava River Valley and onto the field of Dejvice, the dreariness emanating from the abandoned latrine reaches its climax. The wind presses on the rotted wood, disturbing the still of the evening with a creaking noise, thereby imbuing this once glorious place with still greater melancholy. Only when hikers trek to St. Matthew or into the Šárka Valley does the abandoned latrine enjoy an occasional use. However, these visits occur only seldom and are devoid of any glory. By evening, the visitors have disappeared, and then follows a quiet night and an even more disconsolate morning.

The latrine stands there in a state of abandonment, harboring bitterness on the empty drill grounds.

What happened to those times when companies could be heard approaching one after another? The final shots sounded from the men's rifles, and countless steps were heard, followed by a curt command: "Unbuckle belts!"

Then the marching of the company faded away and individual deserters arrived. In delight, they enjoyed peace and quiet under the vast sky, and as they departed, they took a pencil to the planks, to leave their mark—pairing their thoughts with appropriate drawings.

Every now and then, a hostile sentry wearing a white cap would wander past, and then they sat there on the beams, friend next to enemy, exchanging their views.

Ah, yes! Such activity has evaporated—vanished in much the same way as many things in the water of that stream.

*

While out for a stroll, a retired major by the name of Zettel chanced upon the abandoned latrine.

Atop one of the plum trees with downward-bending branches sat a crow. Its presence suited this place, and the retired major gazed gloomily at the field and at the abandoned latrine.

He continued further up the mountain, so as to reach a better vantage point from which to view the surrounding area. He paused at the top and looked down at the field, through the delicate and translucent afternoon clouds. Years ago, he had ridden there every morning, high upon his steed, before companies of soldiers. The brash blue of the military was everywhere, the trumpets blared, commands sounded, cries and curses were heard, and the horses galloped about wildly. And today, below, the abandoned latrine, which had once known so much activity…

As he descended the mountain, Major Zettel felt wistful, like one who reflects on a friend deceased, on youth lost, or on money squandered.

The major was in a hurry. The feelings of melancholy exerted a physiological effect on his body.

With pep in his step and his jacket unbuttoned, he approached the abandoned latrine.

There, on the beams, sat a quite ordinary man, a civilian—a wayfarer, by all appearances.

The retired Major Zettel made a distressed motion and fell into the ditch dug by the engineers of yore.

His military heart had broken, for it could not endure the thought of an ordinary civilian emptying his bowels into a military latrine.

Abandoned Latrine

The quick-witted wayfarer inspected the major's pouch and departed happily with his watch and wallet.

And today, when the dark of night sets in, the ghost of the retired major can still be found seated on the beams of the abandoned latrine, and heart-rending cries can be heard.

1912